Kids love reading
Choose Your Own Adventure®!

CHECK OUT CHOOSE YOUR OWN NIGHTMARE:
EIGHTH GRADE WITCH • BLOOD ISLAND • SNAKE INVASION

YOU MIGHT ALSO ENJOY THESE BESTSELLERS...

CHOOSE YOUR OWN ADVENTURE®

SPIES: NOOR INAYAT KHAN

RANA TAHIR

ILLUSTRATED BY LAURENCE PEGUY
COVER ILLUSTRATED BY MIA MARIE OVERGAARD

CHOOSECO
WAITSFIELD, VERMONT

Choose Your Own Adventure Spies: Noor Inayat Khan
© 2020 Chooseco LLC, Waitsfield, Vermont. All Rights Reserved.

Book design: Stacey Boyd, Big Eyedea Visual Design

For information regarding permission, write to:

CHOOSECO
P.O. Box 46
Waitsfield, Vermont 05673
www.cyoa.com

ISBN-10: 1-937133-37-0
ISBN-13: 978-1-937133-37-5

Names: Tahir, Rana, author. | Peguy, Laurence, illustrator.
Title: Spies. Noor Inayat Khan / Rana Tahir ; illustrated by Laurence Peguy.
Other Titles: Noor Inayat Khan | Choose your own adventure. Spies.
Description: Waitsfield, Vermont : Chooseco, [2020] | Interest age level: 007-012. | Summary: "YOU are the world's first Spy Princess, Noor Inayat Khan ... World War II changed your life, but also showed the world you were one of the bravest women who ever lived. You left your easy life behind to spy for the Resistance as a British secret agent, and became the first female radio operator who entered Nazi-occupied France. Did the lessons of your life prepare you for the realities of war?"--Provided by publisher.
Identifiers: ISBN 1937133370 | ISBN 9781937133375
Subjects: LCSH: Khan, Noor Inayat, 1914-1944--Juvenile fiction. | Women spies--Great Britain--Juvenile fiction. | World War, 1939-1945--Secret service--Great Britain--Juvenile fiction. | World War, 1939-1945--Secret service--Great Britain--Fiction. | Spy stories. | CYAC: Khan, Noor Inayat, 1914-1944--Fiction. | Women spies--Great Britain--Fiction. | LCGFT: Action and adventure fiction. | Choose-your-own stories.
Classification: LCC PZ7.1.T328 Spn 2020 | DDC [Fic]--dc23

Published simultaneously in the United States and Canada

Printed in Canada

10 9 8 7 6 5 4 3 2 1

To all the quiet kids who want to make trouble.

BEWARE and WARNING!

This book is different from other books. YOU and you alone are in charge of what happens in this story.

Your name is Noor Inayat Khan, and you have a secret royal heritage. You live with your family in a beautiful home in France, where you write poetry and children's books. You study music and can speak many languages. Everything for you and your family changes with World War II.

News hits that the Nazis have come to France and YOU have a big decision to make. You were raised with pacifist beliefs but you see how important it is to help with the war efforts. Will you escape to India, your father's homeland? Or will you remain in Europe and find a way to help with the war? You will also make choices that determine YOUR own fate in the story. Choose carefully because the wrong choice could end in disaster—even death. But don't despair. At any time, YOU can go back and make another choice, and alter the path of your fate . . . and maybe even history.

You rush toward your childhood home in Suresnes, France, a luxury suburb of Paris. Mansions line the streets, flanked by gorgeously full trees and birds singing in the sunlight. The day is hot, but that is not why a bead of sweat slides down your face.

The morning started off normally. You had some errands to run: groceries for dinner, buying a new notebook to write your latest stories and poems in. You were just leaving your favorite bookstore when you heard two women talking, asking each other frantically if the Nazis had reached Paris. They had heard gossip but did not know the facts. The radio news broadcast will start in five minutes, and you want to be home in time to hear it. You round the corner, your eyes darting left and right.

You reach the bottom step of your home, run up the stairs, and burst inside. Your younger brother, Vilayat, sits at the kitchen table, in clear view of the family radio. You take a breath, say nothing, and sit next to him. When the minute hand hits twelve, he turns on the radio.

When the broadcast ends, Vilayat turns off the radio. You both look at each other in shock.

"Is it true, Vilayat? The Nazis are in France?" you ask your brother. He does not answer you, just strokes his beard, deep in thought. "Vilayat?" you repeat.

Vilayat is staring at the portrait of your father and mother on the wall.

Turn to the next page.

2

"It is true, Noor," says Vilayat quietly. You feel
a quiver of fear run down your spine. You've been
listening to the news on the radio every day with
your family. The Germans, led by Adolf Hitler, have
been invading neighboring countries. They started
with Poland last year, and now, after a surprise
attack, the radio announced that France is losing.
France is your home, and a part of your heart. You
are sad and scared.

"You heard the radio same as me." Vilayat looks
at you, a look you know all too well. It is the same
look he would give you as kids when he wanted to
hear a story or go on an adventure together in the
gardens. "You know what this means. We need a
plan to escape."

"A plan to escape?" You are quiet. You and
Vilayat are outsiders here in France, and your
family's wealth will no longer ensure your safety.
All your life, you've written stories about adventures
other children might go on, children who do not
live the quiet, protected life you do. Now you will
need to be brave and act on these fantasies.

"We need to leave tonight, before there is any
threat on our safety." Vilayat gives you a decided
look. He is determined.

"And abandon our home?"

"We have to, Noor." You know he is doing the
right thing. "We won't be safe here. You've heard
what they are doing in Belgium?"

Go on to the next page.

You nod. The Nazis set up puppet governments and a Gestapo police force to crush any resistance. But people still resisted. You feel a pang of want in your chest. Could you be one of the resisters?

"Where would we go?" you ask Vilayat.

"We could go to London? Maybe meet up with some of Baba's friends?"

You nod. It is a good choice to seek out your father's friends. You lived in London before moving to Paris. You lean back on the table, something sharp hits your side. It's a copy of your book, *Twenty Jataka Tales*. In it are stories from India you grew up hearing. When you wrote it, you wanted to bring those tales to Europeans. You jump up. You have an idea!

"What about India?" you ask Vilayat. "We would be safe there, and we could find Baba's family, see our cousins." A warm feeling fills your chest as you recall India.

Vilayat frowns. "I want to go to London so I can stay close to the news here. If we're in India, we'll be too far away to do anything for our home." He is right. Going to London means you can maybe help. Vilayat is stubborn; going to India means saying goodbye to him.

If you choose to make your way to India, turn to the next page.

If you choose to escape with Vilayat, turn to page 11.

"We'll be arriving at our destination in an hour!" the captain's voice booms. You take in another deep breath of the sea air. In your heart you feel a little sadness that the journey is over. You loved being on the ocean.

You heard many stories about India from your father growing up. Even though you are a Sufi like your father, you always loved the Buddhist and Hindu stories full of beautiful, smart, and mischievous creatures and deities who all learned lessons about truth, honesty, kindness, and bravery.

You look at the letters in your hand and smile. They are all from your old friend Adil. Your parents were close; he and his family even came to Paris to visit you once as kids. You would write letters to each other all the time, but of course life got busier as you both got older and eventually the letters slowed to a stop. Now you'll surprise him with a visit!

The ship's horn blares loudly as it pulls up to the dock. All the ship's passengers are out on deck looking over the edge. Hundreds of people are gathered on land! Some are waiting for their loved ones to arrive, waving up at the ship; some walk hurriedly to other parts of the docks, baggage boys trailing behind them carrying suitcases; down the other way you can see regiments of soldiers readying themselves to go off and fight for the British. Even here the war in Europe is apparent.

Turn to page 6.

You wonder what your father would think. He spoke out against the British control of India, where the British Raj has ruled for almost one hundred years. The East India Company, which your father told you was also controlled by the British military, controlled India for one hundred years before that. Now Indian people risk their lives to free the people of France, Belgium, Poland, and other European nations in the war. But what about their own freedom?

"Time to disembark!" The captain's voice booms again. You gather your belongings. You didn't bring much with you, just a suitcase and small handbag. You smile at the large boxes some drag along with them. When you step off the ship you are hit with how different everything is. The ocean smell tangles with savory and sweet smells of spices from the nearby street food vendors, and smoky incense. You catch a few words of English occasionally, but mostly you hear the musical notes of Marathi, Hindi, Urdu, and Gujarati.

"*Bhai.*" You call a young bag carrier near you brother out of respect. "Where is the train station?" The boy gives you directions quickly, then gets back to his work. Adil's family lives in Lahore, and you'll have to catch a train to get there.

You hear your tummy rumble as you pass by a man standing over a big pot that smells sweet. "*Kulfi! Kulfi!*" the man calls out.

Go on to the next page.

Kulfi! You laugh and clap your hands with excitement. Your father always talked about *kulfi*—he would say it was like ice cream, but better. You can't resist, handing the man some rupees with one hand and taking the *kulfi* on a stick with the other. You take a few steps away and then take a bite. "Mmmm . . ." You can't help but say it out loud as the flavors of cardamom and saffron burst in your mouth. Heavenly!

"Karo ya maro!" you hear a crowd shout. You look over, still eating the *kulfi*. A crowd has gathered, chanting slogans and holding signs. *Karo ya maro?* It takes you a second to translate: "Do or die!" It's a resistance slogan! You realize they are protesting British rule; your father supported Indian independence wholeheartedly. You want to look at the protest, but then remember you still haven't gotten a ticket to Lahore.

*If you choose to head to the train station,
turn to the next page.*

*If you choose to watch the protest,
turn to page 19.*

8

You learn at the train station that you cannot get to Lahore until the next day.

Bombay is bustling, and you are very tired from your travels. You decide to find a place to sleep for the night.

After an hour of searching, you find a boarding house for women. It's clean and you can afford a room for yourself. Meals are served downstairs in a community dining hall. You wash your face and hands and then head down.

There are rows and rows of short wooden tables, and cushions to sit on. Most of the seats are taken by women chatting and laughing.

You find a seat at the far end of the room just as the meal is being served, rice with a choice of chicken or vegetables, and side dishes of cooling yogurt and cucumbers, and something that looks like a spinach dish with a kind of cheese inside and a side of warm thick bread.

You look around you, unsure of how to start. The other women begin serving themselves and you watch them carefully rip the bread and use it to spoon up the spinach dish or gather rice with their fingertips and delicately eat. A slightly older woman takes pity on you, seeing the confusion on your face. There is something about her that looks familiar. She points to a mixture of yogurt and cucumbers, then the rice dish, the spinach dish, and the bread. "*Raita, biryani, palak paneer, naan.*" She is teaching you the names.

Turn to page 10.

"Thank you," you reply in English. "I mean, *shukriya*." You blush, hoping you pronounced it right.

"You're welcome," the woman replies in English.

"Oh! You speak English?" You are glad, but also feel silly, because of course some people here would know English.

"Yes, I lived in Europe for a time. Actually, you look quite familiar—my name is Priya Chatterjee."

"Oh my goodness!" you beam. "I thought you looked familiar! It's me, Noor Khan!"

"Inayat Khan's daughter?" She looks shocked. You fill Priya in on what has happened since she left. You tell Priya about the war.

"I'm very sorry." She shakes her head and clicks her tongue. "That is a terrible thing to happen to one's home. And why have you come to India?"

You tell Priya you are here to see your friend Adil.

"I didn't know you and Adil still spoke." Priya looks at you quizzically.

"We don't!" You answer too quickly and blush. "I was hoping to surprise him."

"Adil is a good man, but he's in some serious trouble." Priya hesitates and looks at you harder, as if she is deciding something about you. "I know you want to help him, but I need you to prove it first."

Turn to page 15.

You agree to join Vilayat in London, but the war reaches you there, just months after your arrival. At first, while it was clear the threat of the Nazis put everyone on edge, there was still peace. Vilayat went off to join the Royal Air Force as a minesweeper as soon as your family was settled in their new place. While you were working on building a new life in the United Kingdom, he was in training to defend the world against Nazis.

Today, you are on your way to meet your friend Jane in Falmouth, Cornwall, your new home. Sirens blare. For a moment, everyone on the street freezes in fear. The Nazis are coming. An air raid is about to happen. You need to seek shelter.

You rush with throngs of people for a place to hide from the bombs. There are so many people trying to crowd through a small door, down the stairs, and into the basement, you worry that if you trip you'll be trampled.

The ground shakes harder, and you hear the boom of the bombs coming closer. The few children stuck in the basement with you start to cry, their parents gently shushing them. You feel like the war followed you. Only a few weeks had passed when the Blitz began. Docks are a target, and Falmouth has many.

Turn to the next page.

Ten minutes pass with no sound and no shaking, then the all clear comes. Everyone straightens up. Everyone tries to pretend that life is normal again. You get up from your spot and make it up the stairs.

When you step outside, the air is thick with smoke. You pull your shirt over your nose. Ambulances wail as they plow through the streets looking for casualties.

You feel a spark light inside of you. A woman in a uniform stands on the corner holding flyers. Her hair is pulled back into a neat bun, and she carries herself proudly. "Join the Women's Auxiliary Air Force! Fight for our freedom! Fight for the world!"

You are tired of feeling helpless. But you're also a pacifist. You believe that things should be resolved peacefully. Fighting is always a violent act. You take a step back.

"Oh now, don't walk away. Here," she hands you a flyer. "My name is Vera Atkins."

"My name is Noor."

"It's good to meet you, Noor. Listen, we're looking for women to join our forces. We can't leave it all up to the men. Lord knows they need our help!" She cracks a smile at her own joke. "Take a flyer, we're having a meeting soon. You'll see how helpful you can be."

Turn to page 14.

14

"Helpful?" You repeat the word. You want to be helpful so desperately, but could you ever pick up a gun? Could you really choose violence, even to support a cause you believe in? Jane is a friend of yours who is also a writer. Your planned meeting with her today was to use your mighty pens to make change in the world. Isn't that something you're better at?

If you choose to meet Jane and discuss writing, turn to page 17.

If you choose to join the fight by joining the Women's Air Force, turn to page 24.

"I will tell you what you need to know—if you do me a favor," Priya whispers sternly, "to prove your loyalty to him."

"What is the favor?"

"Shh! Don't talk so loudly. You never know who is listening." She looks around quickly. "My uncle works for the British Raj and for that he's become very wealthy, but that hasn't stopped him from his greed. When my parents passed, he took my inheritance. I don't care about most of it, but there's one thing—a ruby necklace my mother gave me—and I want you to get it back for me."

"Me? How can I—"

Turn to the next page.

16

"My cousin, his daughter, is getting married. Her *shaadi* is today. I'd go myself, but I wasn't invited. My uncle will be too busy with the preparations to notice you, though. Be warned, the British see him as an important asset and keep his home under guard most of the day but less so at night. If you get it for me, I can tell you where they are keeping Adil, but you must act quickly. I'm worried that with any delay my uncle will move the necklace to another location or sell it."

You feel you have no choice but to agree. How else will you get more information to see Adil? What did she mean when she said he is being "kept" somewhere? Priya gives you the address and you head over after finishing your meal.

The house is large and beautiful. Strings of flowers adorn the large walls. From across the street, you can see the *mandap* they've constructed for the bride and groom to sit under. Servants hurry in and out of the home, carrying decorations, dishes of food, and lots of sweets. The British guards keeping watch barely even look their way.

Priya wants me to hurry, you think to yourself, and of course wherever Adil is, he's probably itching to get out of there as fast as possible. Still, you are worried about the guards and wonder if waiting till late at night when there are fewer of them will be simpler. You weigh your options.

If you choose to sneak in with the wedding, turn to page 33.

If you decide to break in at night, turn to page 50.

You decide your writing is what you can offer the world, even during wartime. Jane, your friend and now agent, is bubbly and kind and manages to keep a smile on her face even with the war going on around you. Today, you are at a press conference she has arranged for your new book.

"Ms. Khan! Ms. Khan! How does it feel to be one of the most celebrated writers today?" a reporter asks from the press floor.

"I feel there is so much I can do with my platform. And of course, I love to write and am thrilled people enjoy reading what I create."

"Ms. Khan!" Another reporter jumps up. "Recently in an interview with *Punch* magazine you made some critical comments against the Nazi regime. German sympathizers have called for a boycott of your work. What is your response?"

"I stand by my statements," you say firmly. "It is clear what kind of a threat the Nazis pose to the world; I'm honestly shocked there could be any sympathizers left. Frankly, they should be ashamed of themselves." The crowd applauds wildly.

It's the speaking events you love most. Since Vilayat went off to join the war, you try to do your small part by entertaining the returning troops with readings and, whenever you get the chance, openly criticizing Nazi ideas. You know it's not the same as being in the battle, but you feel proud of your small part in helping.

The End

You drop your hands to your side. No matter what, you are your father's daughter.

"I can't believe you would side with the Nazis, Renee. I just can't."

Renee looks at you, stunned. In the pale light of the moon she looks like she did when she was younger—her head down, hair covering her face. Renee was always the shy girl, the girl who seemed always lost. You see her fists clench harder until she finally releases them.

"How can you just give up?" she asks.

"I'm not giving up. But I won't hurt someone who I once considered a friend."

"I . . ." Renee starts, but is interrupted by a sharp banging on the door. She looks out the window. "Gestapo!" She pauses, then without looking at you says, "Go. Run out the back, I will point them in the wrong direction so you can get away."

All you can do is nod and run.

The war seems like a lifetime away as you walk down the street in Falmouth again. It took SOE about a week to get you out. Then after you were done debriefing Buckmaster and Vera, you headed straight for your family. They were overjoyed to see you. You also were able to get a letter out to Vilayat. Now you write him almost every day.

The weather turns colder. The Nazi air raids continue. It almost feels like before you left. Almost but not quite. When you look at yourself in the mirror, you can see how much it's changed you. You are still trying to live with those changes.

The End

You decide the protest isn't something to be missed. You can always catch a train to Lahore later. You head closer to listen. The main speaker, a frail man in modest clothing and spectacles, has just finished his speech. The crowd is cheering and chanting the resistance call, *Karo ya maro! Karo ya maro!* You nudge someone next to you and ask, "Who was that man?"

"That's Gandhi-ji, of course!" she says, then turns away and continues chanting. Gandhi! You know all about his nonviolent teachings and civil disobedience. He is revolutionary!

"Gandhi-ji is wrong!" you hear someone say. You turn to see a group of people chatting by a small shop. "Nonviolence hasn't gotten us anywhere! I think Bose has the right idea," the man continues. The crowd is dispersing, and you decide to join the conversation.

"I understand your point," you gently interject, "but hasn't Gandhi's way been creating change? Shouldn't we give nonviolence and peace a chance to work?"

"Yes," a woman nods. "She is right—absolutely right! This way is working, so we shouldn't be rocking the boat any further."

You are fascinated by the conversation! France did not often carry the news about protests. And of course, once the war began, all other topics were pushed aside.

"So, who do you support?" the woman asks.

"I haven't joined any group yet. I've just arrived in India."

Turn to the next page.

"Gandhi-ji! Gandhi-ji!" the woman calls out and runs toward Gandhi, who emerges with an entourage of followers. "Excellent speech!"

"Thank you," he says as he presses his palms together and slightly bows. More people flock toward him, and you are carried in the wave. His supporters clamor around him, asking questions and singing his praises. He patiently makes time for each of them.

You look at this tiny man in wonder. He's not particularly striking in any way; in fact, he could probably easily blend into the background if he weren't taking up the struggle for freedom. You admire that. It makes you think about how you could be an influence on the world.

Although you have come to India to seek out Adil and rekindle your friendship, you feel compelled to follow Gandhi right now.

Go on to the next page.

"I would like to join your group. I was raised to believe in nonviolence, and I think your way of protest could change the world." You step forward as you speak.

"It's not that easy." A towering figure with a thick long beard steps toward you.

"Who are you?" Everyone seems in awe of this man.

"Everyone knows Aryan!" someone from the crowd shouts.

"And I know everyone," Aryan grunts, "but I don't know you." He eyes you suspiciously.

"My name is Noor Inayat Khan."

Aryan snorts. "You want to be a part of us? Prove it. We are starting another hunger strike in protest. Let's see how much this cause means to you."

Turn to the next page.

You survived day five of the hunger strike, barely. All the strikers are invited to stay with Gandhi in a large house.

You share your room with some other women strikers and their children. Of course, the children are not striking—being too young—and this only makes it worse for you as you watch them munch on their meals and slurp down goodies all day.

"Oh, Noor," one of the other women says, stepping into the room, "Leila made a big mess and I need to go clean it up. Do you mind staying in the kitchen and watching the stove for me? Thank you!" And before you can say a word, she disappears.

It's as if someone is cooking for an army. You smell the plates of savory vegetarian dishes—most of the occupants of the house being Hindu—and delightful round and square sweets that are piled on top of one another.

"This isn't fair!" you whine.

You shake yourself alert. You need to be mature. The strike is to show the British how much you would sacrifice for freedom. It's to show the world your dedication to the cause. It's not about starving, it's about perseverance despite how hard things get. But right now, things seem too hard. Here you are all alone in a kitchen full of delicious-smelling things you can't eat. You perk up.

I'm all alone, you think to yourself. *No one else is here.*

If you choose to sneak a bite, turn to page 102.

If you choose to stick with the hunger strike, turn to page 39.

You want to help battle the evil that is the Nazis. You want to be part of saving the world! You take the flyer from Vera. "I'll be there," you commit.

You run to find the nearest red telephone booth and call Jane to cancel, apologizing. A clock somewhere chimes in the distance. It's already time for the meeting.

You head down the narrow streets, whipping past everyone.

"Hello again!" a voice calls, and you see Vera, waving. "I'm glad you decided to come back!"

"I thought about what you said, about being helpful," you tell her. "I want to do something."

Vera nods understandingly.

Weeks pass by. The training is grueling. Your instructor, Kenneth, pushes you to the edge each day. There are physical tests, combat training, and tests of the mind. Kenneth is a gruff man, and you suspect he doesn't like you.

Kenneth grumbles as he walks up and down the line. "You!" He points directly at you. "And you!" He points at Elizabeth, whom you befriended during training. You both step forward from the line of trainees.

"You will face each other in hand-to-hand combat." He taps his clipboard with his pen. "I will be taking notes that will go in your permanent file. Your opponent is your enemy. You need to beat them to ensure your mission's success. Countless lives are depending on you to succeed and keep your location a secret."

Turn to page 26.

You and Elizabeth face each other. She is a head taller than you, but you know you're faster. Elizabeth jumps first, lunging at you. You dodge and give her a swift knock on her back. She can't get up. You wait for Kenneth to blow his whistle and declare your victory!

"Kill her," he grunts.

"What?" You spin around. "No. I can't!"

"If you can't pretend to kill a fake enemy here, how can anyone on your team trust you out in the field?" he growls.

"No. I won't do it." You help Elizabeth up as Kenneth grumbles angrily and writes furiously on his clipboard.

Kenneth determines you are not cut out for the work, but you think he's wrong. You march into the office and walk confidently up to the colonel in charge, a man called Buckmaster.

"Sir, I know that you need agents in France who speak French. I am fluent, and France is my home. I would like the chance to do something for her."

"Excuse me?" Colonel Buckmaster is clearly affronted. He takes three steps away from you. "I beg your pardon?"

Vera steps out from an office, looking surprised.

"What's going on here?" she asks.

"I'm asking for another chance to prove myself, ma'am. I want to go to France." You look her directly in the eye.

Go on to the next page.

Buckmaster looks at you, then at Vera, then at you again, then Vera. He lets out a sigh. "Very well. But she's your responsibility."

Vera then takes you by the arm and leads you to another part of the building. "Do you know what SOE does?" she asks, opening the door to a room with a desk.

"Radio?" you gasp when Vera shows you the machine.

"We need agents to send and receive coded communications—but you'll also be expected to fight, to sabotage enemy facilities and weapons, to capture important targets."

Vera pulls out a notebook and hands it to you. "This radio and this notebook are for you and you alone. You must never let anyone find it or take it from you."

You grip the book tightly. "I understand."

"Now there are four rules for being able to tell if a message is real or fake. Number one, every communication must have the correct control message: The fog is in London. Number two, no word you use will ever be seven letters long. Number three, the coded symbols are always scrambled: a control letter will be radioed to you in Morse code. And finally, number four, you can only use your codename, Madeleine, when sending a message. Are you following me?"

You nod.

Turn to the next page.

"Good." She continues, "Now here's how coding works. Once you have received the control letter, you need to fill in the symbol chart. For example, if the control letter is A the chart is filled in like this." She draws a picture:

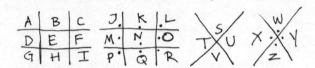

"If the control letter was Q, you would start the chart there." She draws another picture:

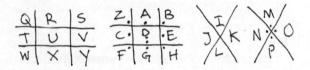

"That way, the symbols are always changing, so the Nazis will not figure out what symbol connects to what letter. Now, here's how we make words. Each 'box' symbolizes a certain letter. For example, your name. Here's your name if the control letter is A." She draws out your full name.

"And here's what it would look like if the control letter is Q. See the difference?"

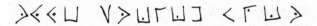

"These codes are how you will send and receive messages. Now we're going to practice. Your control letter is H. The message is 'SOE notices are confidential, the fog is in London, Madeleine.'" You set pen to paper.

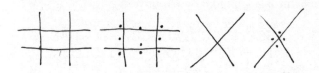

"Check to see if your code matches the correct answer."

Use the space below to practice the code.

Turn to the next page.

30

"Here." Vera hands you a paper with the correct code on it.

⌐⌐⊐ 7⊓ヨ∪∧ラ∟ ラ∪ラ
∧∪7< ∪∨ラ7ヨ∪ラ⊡

ヨ⌐ラ<⌐∧ ∪∟ ∪7 ⊡⌐7∨⌐7
⌐ラ∨ラ⊡ラ∪7ラ

"Now look closely at the message. Without looking back at the rules for messages. Can you tell if this is a legitimate code or not?"

**SOE NOTICES ARE CONFIDENTIAL
THE FOG IS IN LONDON MADELEINE**

Go on to the next page.

Vera points to the code. "It's not a legitimate code because the word NOTICES has seven letters in it. See how tricky this can be?"

Vera runs you through the ringer with practice and training sessions. You learn how to properly care for your radio, how to line the aerial antenna to boost a signal, and other important maintenance tricks.

"Remember, your radio is your lifeline. Without it, you can't contact us for help," Vera warns you over tea one afternoon. "It also makes you a target. Just like we can pinpoint your signal, so can Nazis. So don't stay in one place for too long. Finish your messages and then move to a safe location." Vera pauses.

"Noor, it's not too late to back out."

Your fear must show on your face because the next thing Vera says is, "It's not that I don't think you're capable. I have full confidence in you. It's just—"

Turn to the next page.

Vera bites her lip and then says, "It's just that the life expectancy of this job is quite short."

"You mean people don't last long." Neither of you has touched the tea. You watch a small ribbon of steam rise out of the teapot.

"Yes, especially in Paris. We don't know why, but our agents are often captured or killed very early on." Vera puts her hands on the table, then on her lap, then back on the table. She is clearly nervous.

"Why are you telling me this?"

"Because I consider you a friend, and I've watched too many agents go on their missions wondering if they really know what's in store for them. I want you to make the decision with all of the facts." She squeezes your hand.

You consider what she says. You could go back to your writing. But—you look up at Vera—you know there is a part of you that can't sit by and do nothing. You think of what your old instructor Kenneth asked: Will you be trustworthy in the field, when the danger is real and no longer pretend? You know whatever decision you make now, there is no going back.

If you choose to go back to your writing career, turn to page 17.

If you choose to continue, turn to page 42.

You decide to infiltrate the wedding during the day for Priya, but you'll need different clothing first. You run to a nearby clothing shop, gently pulling apart the soft cloth drapes that act as a door. Along the walls are shelves filled with beautiful glittering cloths waiting to be stitched into delicate, graceful dresses. You need to look like you fit in with the rest of the wedding attendees, but you don't want to stand out. Of course, there's no time to get measured and have something made especially for you, and you let out a small whimper when you see a beautiful blue chiffon cloth with gold thread embroidery on the shelf.

Instead, you look at the opposite wall where there are ready-made dresses awaiting purchase. You pick a pale green *shalwar kamiz* that develops into a bright pink. There are small sequins and mirrors sewn into the *dupatta*. You take it off the hanger and walk up to the storekeeper, paying her and asking if you can change in the back of the store. She is surprised by your request, but shrugs and lets you head back there. When you emerge, you can't help but steal a glance in the nearby mirror. It's a beautiful dress, though it is more on the plain side. You wrap your *dupatta* around your head and face, only revealing your eyes. Then you head toward the servants at the wedding.

You take a plate of sweets from one of them and then line up to get into the house. It works! No one notices you, and now you're inside.

Turn to the next page.

The inside of the home is more spectacular than the outside. There are three floors centered around a courtyard, all of them open and airy and decorated with brand-new candles, fresh flowers, and colorful drapes that glitter. In one corner of the courtyard a band sets up their instruments. The *mandap*, the four curtained pillars the bride and groom will wed under, stands in the center, brightly colored and decorated with small, delicate petals that curl around each pillar. Beside it is a small pyre for a fire.

Everyone is working quickly: some people braid more flowers onto string; some arrange the food on the buffet table; others sweep the floors and prepare baskets of rose petals to greet the bride and groom. You try not to let yourself become mesmerized by the display. You have a job to do.

Priya said the necklace would be somewhere close to her uncle. She knows his office is on the second floor of the home.

Turn to page 37.

You head up the stairs, trying not to look out of place. You pass by a room and catch a glimpse of the bride—she is dressed in a regal orange *lehnga* with embroidered gold lotus flowers. It sweeps the floor as she paces. Her lips are painted a blush pink, and her eyes darkened with kohl. Delicate henna designs cover her hands and feet, winding up to her elbows and ankles. Gold jewelry adorns her arms, her neck, her nose, her ears. She is a vision. She is also clearly nervous. You smile, wondering if your mother was this nervous on her own wedding day to your father. You quickly pass by the door before someone notices you there.

You find the right room. Inside is a grand mahogany desk with a matching chair cushioned with silk, antique wood furniture intricately carved, and a large gold-framed portrait of King George VI. You step in, carefully rifling through the drawers and cabinets. Nothing! Nothing! You can't find the ruby necklace anywhere in the room.

"There you are!" comes a woman's voice. You jump and turn around. It is the bride, so close to you that you can see her delicate henna designs. "I was hoping someone would come soon, you really took forever to get here!"

Turn to the next page.

"I—I," you freeze. You can feel the blood drain from your face.

"Here," she comes up to you, her hands clasped in front of her. "Take it quickly!" She opens her hands to reveal the ruby necklace. "Tell Priya I'm so sorry and I wish she could be here with me." Her eyes glisten with tears.

"I will." You bow your head and quickly run out the door, down the stairs, and out into the street.

Turn to page 45.

You grab a stool, set it in the farthest corner of the kitchen, and sit there staring at the stove. "No! No! No! No! No!" you sing to yourself.

"No, what?" Aryan walks in.

"Nothing. I'm just watching the stove for someone."

"Oh." He looks at you in the far corner, away from any food. "I always hated kitchen duty during hunger strikes." He pulls up another stool and sits with you. "The smell would drive me crazy."

At that moment, your stomach rumbles loudly. You look at Aryan, then at your stomach, then back at him, then your stomach again. You look at him one more time and then you both burst into laughter!

"I'm surprised," Aryan says between laughs. "I honestly didn't think you'd make it."

"I almost didn't," you admit. Aryan just nods, and you can tell he appreciates your honesty.

"Well I'm impressed, and I know the others will be too." You chitchat to distract yourselves from the hunger.

Turn to the next page.

40

Days later, when the hunger strike finally ends, Gandhi hosts a celebration and you're invited to attend.

"Ah, Noor! Just who I was looking for," Aryan says. "I'd like to introduce you to someone." He leads you through the intimate gathering into another room. On the ground you see Gandhi sitting, smiling.

"Mr. Gandhi!" You suddenly don't know what to do with your hands. Should you bow? Curtsy? "It's an honor!"

"Ms. Khan." Gandhi motions for you to have a seat. You drop down to the ground with no grace. He only smiles mirthfully. "Aryan has told me so much about you. It's not every day someone impresses him."

"I—" You don't know what to say. Mercifully, Aryan steps in.

"I told him a little bit about your background, what you shared with me." Aryan sits between you and Gandhi.

"Yes, I'm sorry to hear about your home in Paris," Gandhi replies solemnly. "I understand your brother is fighting in Europe."

"Yes, he joined the British Air Force after fleeing to London." You feel a sadness well up in your heart. You worry about Vilayat.

"I wonder how you feel about the war," Gandhi continues. "You know many Indians are fighting as well?"

Go on to the next page.

"Yes," you say, thinking back to the day you arrived in Bombay. "I noticed many Indian soldiers departing at the docks when I first arrived. I suppose I didn't feel as odd about it then as I do now."

"What do you mean?" Aryan asks.

"Of course I see the war in Europe as a noble endeavor. All the news about the Nazis makes it clear how evil they are. Not to mention the fact that I have been exiled from my childhood home because of them." You pause. "But, on the other hand, it does feel odd to fight for the freedom of others as part of an army that denies you your freedom in your homeland."

"It's clear you don't like to see others suffering." Gandhi pauses. "I see you are not only intelligent and willful, but you also possess a kind heart."

"Why, thank you?" It comes out as a question.

"I asked you here because I wanted to know if you were interested in perhaps speaking at one of our rallies?"

"Me!" You almost choke. You have done some public speaking in school, of course, and when your book was first published, you did give some readings. But you're not sure you're comfortable becoming the face of a movement. On the other hand, this is another way you can help the cause. Gandhi waits for your answer.

*If you choose to speak at the rally,
turn to page 108.*

If you choose not to speak, turn to page 88.

42

It is test day. This is your chance to prove to Vera that she was right to help you. You sit at your radio and wait for the signal. The message blips by quickly; you catch it. The control letter is W. You pull out your notebook and write down the two codes. It is time to decipher them.

A)

⊓∨ Ⲫ∨⊅ Ⳃ∨Λⴄⵏ⊅ ⊅Ⳃ⌐∃∨Ⲫ⊅Λ∨ ⅂

⊓⌐∨∨◻ ⱳ⌐ ⊅Ⳃ⌐ Ⳃ∨ⱳ ∃∨ ∃Ⲫ

⅂∨Ⲫ⊓∨Ⲫ

B)

⊅Ⳃ⌐ Ⳃ∨ⱳ ∃∨ ∃Ⲫ ⅂∨Ⲫ⊓∨Ⲫ

Λ⌐⊓⌐⊓ⳂⵏΛ ⅃∨ ⅃◻∃⌐ ⅂◻ΛⵏⲢ

Now you need to determine which code is legitimate. You carefully check each one and then decide.

If you select answer A, turn to page 49.

If you select answer B, turn to page 95.

TAKE ME TO LONDON

You type out the message slowly, but you've made up your mind. The war is dangerous and forces you to make decisions you can't bear living with. You think of everything you've done so far.

WILL DO

You are walking to a meeting in Falwell two weeks later. You think to yourself how funny it is that it all started with a walk to a meeting with a friend. Now, so much time has passed, but here you are again walking to a meeting with Jane, ready to take your writing career more seriously. Your writing has changed since your time in the war. You are changed.

The End

"She just gave it to you?" Priya looks shocked. She gingerly takes the necklace from your hands. "I didn't know she still cared. We were so close growing up." She wipes a tear away. "About Adil," she abruptly changes the subject. "I believe he is in serious trouble for protesting the British rule. I will give you the address of a contact in Amritsar you can trust. Please send her my love."

You nod. There's no time to waste. Adil needs your help. But first you need to see his mother. You hurry toward the train station.

The station's building is huge, eating up the skyline with turrets and high archways. You can't believe it's a station and not a royal palace. You note the delicate woodcarving on all the doors as you enter, and inside, the domed ceilings echo the sounds of the station. You walk to the ticket booth.

"One ticket on the next train to Lahore please."

"The train departs at 4:30 from platform 7." He bows his head slightly. You decide to head to your platform and wait.

"All aboard the Frontier Mail!" the train conductor calls out. The train is overcrowded, and people press closely together. You feel lucky to find a seat next to a window.

The train lets out a loud whistle and pulls away from the platform. People wave their goodbyes; you watch as small children run along the train, waving until the train picks up speed disappears from sight.

Turn to the next page.

The train moves quickly, and you are content to watch the verdant, lush landscapes and mountains fade in and out of view. The greenery here is different from what you are used to. You think of the blue-hued deciduous forests of the French countryside. Here everything is tinged with bright yellows and oranges. Then the landscape changes, becoming arid. You can see the city rise from the earth on the horizon.

"Now arriving in Lahore!" The conductors come through the train cars. You pick up your suitcase and step off the train, then out into the city. Lahore is bustling like Bombay was. Here is the same melody of languages, except Punjabi dominates unlike Bombay with its Marathi tunes. You don't know how far Adil's home is, so you flag down a horse and buggy and tell the driver the address you are going to. The driver nods his head and takes you there.

You love the ride. You can see tea houses overflowing with people. You see the round domes and towers of mosques gleaming in the sun. You get closer to the Lahore Fort, one of the few remnants of the old city before it billowed out into this metropolitan mass. Adil had mentioned he lived in the older part of the city.

Go on to the next page.

Soon enough, the buggy turns off Fort Road and slows to a halt in a narrow alleyway of homes. You thank the driver and pay him some rupees, then take your belongings and stand outside the door. You take a deep breath and knock.

"*Ek* minute!" One minute, a woman calls out from behind the door. The door swings open to an older woman, adjusting the *dupatta* over her head. "*Kon?*" Who?

You recognize her immediately! It's Adil's mother. "Auntie-ji, it's me Noor. I'm—"

"Oh! Noor! Inayat's daughter? Come in, come in! It's been so long!" She ushers you inside and closes the door. You see two floors of open hallways, each room open to the courtyard in the center where you stand now. "When did you get here?"

"I just arrived in Lahore," you say, having a seat on a wicker cot across from Adil's mother. "I was hoping to surprise Adil."

Auntie gives a half-smile, but her eyes darken. "Oh, if you had arrived earlier, maybe he wouldn't have . . ."

"What happened?"

Turn to the next page.

"Oh, my dear," Auntie-ji's voice cracks. "Adil hasn't been home in weeks. He went off to join a protest and I haven't seen him since. I've tried to contact the police and reach out to people who were there, but no one will tell me anything!" She weeps into her hands. Auntie has just confirmed what Priya told you. Adil is in trouble!

"Weeks?" You take a deep breath. "Where did Adil spend his free time?"

"What?" She looks up at you, blinking.

"Did he have a place he liked to go to when he wasn't working?"

"Oh." She understands what you are asking. "One of his best friends is a *chai wallah*—a tea server—at a shop two blocks away. Adil used to spend an hour or so there with his friends after work every day."

You think about your options. In your handbag is the contact Priya gave you, but looking at how distraught Auntie is, you're not sure you should leave Lahore without more information. You don't want to waste any more time. You need to find Adil. You need to help Auntie. You must decide where to start your search.

If you choose to go to the tea shop, turn to page 57.

If you choose to go to the police, turn to page 60.

Gripping the edges of your khaki skirt so tightly your knuckles turn white, you watch as the tests are handed back.

Finally, your test result is on your desk. With a trembling hand you turn it over. FAIL.

"Please, give me one more chance!" you tell Vera. "I know I can do it."

"Noor, you failed. Take this as a sign. Maybe you're not meant for this."

"Vera, I know I can do this. Please. I need you to believe in me. If you won't, Buckmaster will never give me a chance." You look pleadingly into her eyes, refusing to break.

Turn to page 66.

50

You decide not to tempt fate during the wedding. Instead, you wait for the cover of night.

Just as Priya said, most of the guards disappear. The house looks abandoned with everyone asleep and all the lights out. You can see the remnants of the wedding party, flowers and confetti strewn everywhere. By now, the groom has left for his final night apart from his bride.

You measure yourself against the wall. It is high, but with a little boost and a jump, you can pull yourself over. You drag an empty wooden crate against the wall and stand on it. Then, reaching as high as you can, you jump and grab the ledge. You take a breath, dangling from the wall and then pull yourself up. You made it to the top! Now to get down.

You look below, and as luck would have it, an empty buffet table sits right there. The jump down will be easier. You hold yourself from the ledge over the other side, and then drop with a thud onto the buffet table.

"Who is there?" You hear a voice call out. "Hello?"

You see it's a servant. She hasn't seen you yet!

Turn to page 117.

You are on small plane in the dead of night, looking down at France. You and three others sit quietly as the pilot navigates without an interior light. The stars shine magnificently up here.

"We're going to descend now, so hold on tight," the pilot calls back. You feel the plane dip its nose, and everything tilts forward. Then the plane evens out, and you feel a bounce as the wheels touch the ground. You're home.

You are the first off the plane. It takes every bit of control in you not to kiss the ground right there. A tall, slender man approaches you.

"I am Emile. I'm to take you to the location of headquarters. Come quickly."

Turn to the next page.

Winding through the dark streets, you can already see how France has changed. Nothing glows like it used to. When you reach Paris, it becomes worse.

Nazi flags hang from buildings. You can see guards patrolling. Emile moves seamlessly, leading you through the maze of buildings without giving even a hint to the guards. When you turn a corner, you can see the Eiffel Tower looking like a grim monument instead of the fluorescent wonder you love.

"*Voila*! We are here." Emile knocks four times in a rhythm—*knock, knock-knock, knock*—and the door opens. You are ushered inside quickly.

"Get some rest," Emile says. "Your first mission is in the morning."

Turn to page 56.

At the first crack of dawn, you jump out of bed and head downstairs. Emile is waiting.

"Sorry there was no time for the pleasantries last night," he says, shaking your hand. "The night patrols are quite aggressive, so moving quickly at night is important. I'm in charge of the operations here at SOE. And your name is?"

"Noor."

"You mean Madeleine." Emile nods, using your code name.

"Right." You want to kick yourself: rookie mistake.

"I know that you are very familiar with France, so I won't give you directions to your location. You are to go to this house," he points on a map, "and set up the radio there to receive coded messages."

You take off into the streets of Paris, trying to stay unnoticed by any of the guards.

"You there!" A voice bellows. You freeze. "Where are your papers?"

Turn to page 71.

You approach the tea shop. The shop is quaint, basically a hallway, with a radio, small stools, and tables for guests with a stove in the back.

"*Salam*," the owner greets you. You nod and greet him back.

"Just *chai* please." The man grunts at your answer and pours you a cup. "Thank you." You take a sip, pondering your next move. The owner doesn't speak to you at all, he's busy listening to a speech in English on the radio.

Finally, the speech ends. "*Vah, vah,*" the owner shakes his head appreciatively, "that Jinnah knows how to put words together, not as well as Ambedkar, though." You smile and nod at the heavyset man, probably as old as your father would be if he were alive today. His beige *shalwar kamiz* barely hides the stains he's probably amassed over years of running this place. "The problem," the man says, "is that all of Jinnah's speeches are in English! The man needs to learn some Urdu." He lets out an uproarious laugh.

"Do you often listen to the speeches they make?" you ask.

"Of course." He looks affronted. "Everyone should, our futures are being shaped this very moment."

"You sound like my friend Adil," you say, rolling your eyes.

"You're friends with Adil?" His eyes grow grave and serious. "I've never seen you here before . . ."

Turn to the next page.

58

"We're family friends. I've just come from Adil's home where I'm visiting. I've never been to Lahore before."

"These are trying times," he says softly, shaking his head. "That poor boy."

"His mother wants answers," you say, not allowing yourself to break eye contact with him. He wavers under your stare.

"I'm sure she misses him. He was a good boy—"

"Was? You act like he's—"

"He might as well be."

Your lips open to speak but no words come out; you can only blink. "How can I find out what happened to him?"

The man sighs, knowing you won't let go of this. "Talk to them." He nods in the direction of a group of young men whispering to one another. "They are the last people I saw Adil with. His friends, though these days you can never be too sure."

You look over at them. Their eyes dart this way and that. You didn't notice before, but it looks like they're sweating. You remember Adil's mom telling you no one will give answers. You wonder if it would be different if you confront them. Or maybe you should just get closer?

If you choose to talk to them, turn to page 90.

If you choose to eavesdrop on the conversation, turn to page 70.

60

The police station is crowded. You wait for an hour. One officer has done absolutely nothing but read a paper.

"Excuse me," you say as you walk up to the officer. "I'm looking for my friend."

"Go sit and wait to be called," he snaps at you.

"I have been, and it's been an hour, and in that hour, I've watched you do absolutely nothing. So, no, I won't go back and sit down." You hear another couple of officers stifle their laughter. The officer you're speaking to glares at you and puts away his paper.

"What do you want?"

"As I said, Officer . . . ?"

"Kirpal."

"Officer Kirpal, as I said, I'm looking for my friend." You explain the situation, that you've come to India to see Adil, that his mother hasn't seen him in weeks and is worried, and that you've decided to go looking for him.

"Ah, yes. I know that prisoner." Officer Kirpal rubs the tip of his mustache, pretending to consider something. You wonder if this is an officer you can trust.

Go on to the next page.

"Who are you, exactly?" Officer Kirpal sneers, tapping his fingers impatiently on the desk. It's clear he wants to get back to his newspaper and ignore you.

"I'm his friend. I was sent here by his mother. He should be allowed visitors, it's only human," you say through gritted teeth.

"Look miss, I am not here to debate philosophy with you! You want to see him, bring his lawyer with you."

"But he doesn't have a—"

"Not my problem." With that, Officer Kirpal flips open his newspaper, holding it high enough to cover his entire head from your view.

You want to scream, but there's nothing you can do. Dejectedly, you head toward the door. *Causing a scene won't change things for Adil,* you tell yourself. You want to see Adil so much. It's clear no one here will help you. If they did, they would have stepped in by now.

As if on cue, another police officer whispers to you, "Come back tonight. I will leave the door unlocked. You can come in to see your friend." When you turn around, no one is there, but on the floor you notice something odd. You bend down to pick it up; it is a piece of paper with an address in Dhaka. That is Adil's handwriting! You'd recognize it anywhere.

If you choose to head to Dhaka, turn to page 104.

If you choose to break in at night, turn to page 103.

62

"Are you listening?" The guard comes closer. You grab a rock and throw it at him, then run into the house. You need to get your radio and code book; it cannot fall into Nazi hands!

When you finish putting the radio away in its case, the guard is at the door, blocking your exit.

"Hands up now!" His face is beet red, and you can see a vein bulging through his forehead. You rush to the window and throw your radio and book out, but the guard catches you before you can jump after it.

"Augh!" He pulls you by your hair. You kick him hard in the face, blood spurting from his nose. You run toward the stairs, but you feel him barrel into your side and knock you down the stairs. You tumble down, hear a loud crack, and black out.

You are captured by the Nazis and taken to a Nazi prison! Two soldiers drag you out of your cell and down a long hall for another interrogation.

"I will not tell you anything," you say for what seems like the hundredth time. You've been interrogated for hours.

Go on to the next page.

It has been days since you were captured and each day there was an interrogation and starvation. You only got food if you cooperated. Your stomach rumbles loudly.

"I see you are hungry. Shall I bring in some food? For me of course, not you." Your interrogator, Maurice, rings a bell. "Food. Now." He yells at the soldier by the door. Everyone here wears the red bands with the swastika proudly displayed. You wonder if you should tell them that symbol is a Hindu one originally that Hitler stole. Maybe Maurice would choke on his food. You smile at the thought. There is a part of you that is still afraid— you are in the presence of pure evil—but so far, you have given them nothing.

"You've been quite difficult, mademoiselle," Maurice says as he takes a seat in front of you. His dinner, a steak with béarnaise sauce, is brought to him and he eats ravenously. "Your friends, on the other hand, have been quite helpful."

"I don't believe you."

"Then your codename is not Madeleine?" He smiles. Your eyes widen. "We know everything about you, Noor. Or should I call you Bang Away Lulu?"

"You couldn't possibly know that nickname—"

"Unless we have someone from your training days in London? Perhaps we do."

Turn to page 65.

"As I said," Maurice continues, licking some sauce from his fingers, "we know everything about you. And you have information that could be useful to us. If you help us, we can help you and your friends. If you don't—" he slams the blade of his knife straight down into the table.

"I won't—"

"You forget, we know everything about what you've done. The entire spy cell in Paris has been found out.

"Tell us what you know, and you and your friends are safe. Tell us how some of your agents know our messages to them are fake."

You shudder. Telling them the secrets to the code would mean giving them everything.

*If you choose not to cooperate,
turn to page 96.*

*If you choose to give them the information,
turn to page 124.*

66

"Well, you're nothing if not persistent. Fine. I'll go talk to Buckmaster."

Vera walks out of Buckmaster's office, smiling. "You have one more shot, it's another test." She waves the paper in front of you.

You look at the paper and begin your test. It asks you what the three rules for a legitimate code are, how you should decipher the control letter, what name you should use when signing off. You answer all of the questions quickly, and now you are down to the last one. You need to use your knowledge and decipher two codes, then select which one is the legitimate one. The control letter is T.

A)

⅃ᴱᴸ ꓱ∧◻ ꓶA ꓘ ∨∧‹ᏔA‹

‹ᴸ∀∧‹⅃ ᏔA A∧ᴸ ꓱ›

B)

⅃ᴱᴸ ꓱ∧◻ ꓶA ꓘ ∨∧‹ᏔA‹ Ꮤᴸꓱꓶ‹ꓘ‹◻

∧‹Ꮤᴸ‹∧ ꓶꓶ∨∨ ꟻᴸ ∀Ꮜ‹ꓶAᴱᴸᏔ

If you choose answer A, turn to page 95.

If you choose answer B, turn to page 83.

You smile politely as the guard gets closer. "I just can't live without my music."

"Radios are against the rules," he answers.

"I know, and I'm sorry but I simply can't do without my jazz stations."

"I love jazz," he says. "Those Americans do make good music. I'm Friedrich." He tips his hat.

"Jeanne-Marie," you say, giving him a fake name.

"You know what—one music lover to another— let me help you with that." He reaches out to start laying out the aerial antenna.

The guard takes the antenna and starts wrapping it around the tree, even up to some higher branches you couldn't reach!

"How long have you lived in Paris?" he asks.

"All my life."

As he works, the guard continues to chitchat about some things. Finally, after an hour's work, he bids you a friendly farewell.

You head inside. It is almost the rendezvous time for the messages. When you turn on the machine, the signal comes in clear. You let out a big, loud laugh.

Turn to the next page.

You set out your book to record the messages as they come in. The window of opportunity is narrow, and you don't want to miss a single word. A woman's voice comes in clear. You don't know who is on the other side, but you hope it is Vera. There is no way to know.

The messages are swift: troop movements, intelligence needs, coordination requests. Your pen flies across your notebook's pages. When you look outside, you can see the sun setting. It will be dark soon.

Finally, you put down your pen. You quickly get to work taking down the aerial antenna and putting away your machine. You remember Emile's words about the night patrols being quite aggressive.

Now comes the hard part. The SOE safehouse is all the way on the other side of the city.

You wonder, *Would I be safer if I stayed here for the night?*

If you choose to go back to the safehouse, turn to page 74.

If you choose to stay in the abandoned house, turn to page 78.

Before you ask for another cup of tea, the shop owner skillfully pours you one. You choose a seat closer to Adil's friends so you can listen. One of them puts his head down on the table.

"I just can't believe he's gone," he says mournfully.

"Stop talking about Adil as if he were dead," another snaps.

"Enough! What we should be focusing on is finding him."

"What we should have done is watch out for him like we were supposed to in the first place!"

"I was there, remember?" the peacemaker says, his patience running thin. "In any case, he's in the jail."

"Can we really trust that information?"

"Yes," the peacemaker's voice clips. "It's reliable. This is from someone deep on the inside with that British man, Captain Marley. We can't trust the police on this."

You listen longer, but the conversation turns in circles, with the men all squabbling with one another. You finish your tea and walk out of the tea shop, heading toward Adil's home. Maybe it's time to leave Lahore and meet that contact in Amritsar? Or is it time to go to the police?

If you choose to head to the train station, turn to page 72.

If you choose to go to the police station for help, turn to page 60.

You turn slowly and then breathe a sigh of relief. The guard wasn't talking to you. He yanks some documents out of a woman's hands. Then, without warning, he throws them back in her face. As the woman walks away, you notice the yellow Star of David on her coat. You hope she stays safe.

You make it to the location, a large home that seems abandoned. You take the radio inside and set it on a dusty table. You start the machine, trying to get a signal. Instead, you only hear static.

You grab the aerial antenna and head out cautiously. It looks like the coast is clear, so you unravel the antenna and try to loop it around the tree branches, somewhere high up to get the signal.

"Ma'am?" comes a man's voice. You freeze. When you turn around, it is the same guard you saw earlier. "What are you doing?"

Your heart begins to race. The guard is still far enough away that you could make a run for it, but you don't know how far you'll get. He didn't speak harshly. You wonder if you should risk a conversation.

*If you choose to make a run for it,
turn to page 62.*

*If you choose to take a risk on a lie,
turn to page 67.*

72

You approach the Lahore Railway again. When you enter, you head straight to the ticket counter. "I need to leave Lahore today," you tell the clerk.

"Destination?" He points to the train schedule behind him. "There are only three trains going out today."

You read the train schedule and decide to take the 3:30 train to Amritsar. Amritsar is like a fairytale. It's not nearly as big as Bombay or Lahore, and much more rural than you expected. It shares a lot of the same architecture Lahore does; it is a beautiful piece of Punjab. The address you have from Priya is for the Golden Temple. You take a moment to clear your head and plan your next moves.

The temple matches its name perfectly. The gold-plated domes of the Sikh temple shine in the sunlight. You wonder at its beauty and the oddity of the Gothic style clocktower.

"Priya sent you?"

You spin around to see a woman in a green *shalwar kamiz* and blue *dupatta*. She covers her face so you can only see her eyes. "Y-yes," you stammer.

"You don't look like someone she'd usually send. Too frail."

"I'm here about Adil. I need to know what happened to him."

"Not so fast. You want information from me, you need to prove yourself." You want to scream at her, but you can't. You know you need her answers.

Go on to the next page.

"What do I have to do?"

"I need you to help me find the traitor in my midst."

"Why can't you? I don't know anyone here except Adil."

"Obviously if I could, I wouldn't need you." She crosses her arms over her chest and lifts an eyebrow. "Someone who appears to be a protester has been double-crossing us and acting as an informant to Captain Marley. Marley is a British officer and espionage expert. He's been rounding up people from our movement—"

"For independence?" you interrupt.

"Obviously!" Priya's contact snaps. "Captain Marley is capturing people before we can stage our demonstrations. Fear is keeping people from our protests and rallies. Without public support, it will be hard to pressure the British to leave."

"What exactly do you want me to do?"

"I need you to find out who the informant is; the only thing I can tell you is that the informant is either in Lahore or in Dhaka. He works for the police."

"The police?"

"Don't be so surprised. Not everyone is a good guy." She turns away from you and starts walking. "Better move quickly."

If you choose to go back to Lahore, turn to page 60.

If you choose to go to Dhaka, turn to page 104.

The air is crisp and cool as you head to the safehouse. You step into a familiar part of the city and close your eyes, remembering the Paris of your past: the laughter, the music, the smell of food wafting out from the restaurants. You finally wind your way to a darker part of the city, closer to headquarters.

You walk up to the side door and give the special knock you learned: *knock, knock-knock, knock.* The door opens, it's Emile. "Madeleine! You made it! I trust your mission was successful then?"

Crash!

"We're under attack!" you hear someone yell.

A troop of Nazi soldiers bursts through the back door! "Fall back! Fall back!" Emile yells. He pushes you back. "Run, Noor, take your radio and run!"

Screams and gunshots are all around you. As you round the corner, you run headfirst into a Nazi. You slap him with your radio case, knocking him against the wall.

Grabbing your radio, you jump over him and reach the door. When you get outside, another agent pulls you down behind a dumpster, hissing: "Madeleine! Watch out!"

Turn to page 76.

You peer out from behind the dumpster, clutching your radio close to your chest. The whole building is surrounded.

"Things don't look good out here," the agent who pulled you to safety says.

"The best thing right now is to contact London as soon as possible," you say.

"Right," she says as she looks at your radio. She has hers in hand too. The two of you have the only radios left.

"I'm going to make a run for it," the other agent says.

"What? No! There's no way you'll make—" But before you can stop her, she runs. She does not get far.

You look back again. Down an alleyway, you see only one Nazi soldier. You also see a gun within reach.

If you choose to try to run for it, turn to page 85.

If you choose to arm yourself, turn to page 126.

It's too late to cross the whole city. You decide, since you can't go anywhere, to explore the abandoned home. From its huge archways and high ceilings, you can tell that someone very wealthy used to live here.

You walk into what must have once been a grand ballroom, with pink walls and cherubs painted on the ceiling. There are marks on the walls that must have once held up beautiful paintings or mirrors. Those are all gone now. The furniture that is left—a small table and a couple of broken chairs—have mountains of cobwebs on them. It has been a long time since someone has been in this room. In a corner, you see a menorah broken in half.

Just then, you hear your radio frantically going off. You run back to the room, confused. You weren't expecting another message.

The radio beeps out the control letter. You write down T and fill in a new chart, scrambling to keep up with the radio. Then the line goes dead.

THE WEATHER IS FOGGY IN LONDON DANGER COME TO BRUSSELS

You quickly tap back, banging on the keys frantically.

HELLO

HELLO

There is no answer. You are back on your own.

Turn to page 81.

You quickly pack your radio and notebook and head out the door and into the shadows. Just then you see Gestapo running into the building. You barely missed them!

In all the commotion you slip away farther into the shadows. There is an abandoned street, the streetlights flickering on and off, so you time your movements with the light. You make it to the end of the street, turn the corner, and flee. You must make it to Brussels but first you want to check on headquarters.

You hurry down the streets, zigzagging between guards, trying not to bring attention to yourself. As you get closer to headquarters, you start to feel a little calmer. You take a deep breath, realizing for the first time that you had been holding it for so long.

You are only a couple of blocks away when you hear the sirens and gunshots. You drop to your knees, knowing headquarters has been lost.

Turn to the next page.

It takes you a week to leave Paris and make it to the city of Brussels in Belgium. All the while you were deathly afraid of being captured. But you made it. You find a small inn and set up your radio. For the first few days, you wait for hours for a message. But none comes. After a week of feeling isolated and enveloped by the small four walls of your room, you decide to take a gamble and go out.

Despite the heavy Nazi presence, you take in the sights of the city. The tall towers of the Gothic church of St. Michael and St. Gudula loom in the sky in the city center. You remember the church being declared a national historic landmark, years before the Nazi threat ever entered your life. The picture in the newspaper did not do justice to the building. It is massive, making anyone feel small but also a part of something bigger. You wonder if this is what it would feel like to be in the presence of the Taj Mahal, or Amer Fort in India. Sometimes you wonder, when a Nazi guard harasses you or others, if you have made the right choice. It feels so long ago.

But now there is no going back. You return to the radio, sip tea, and wait. You hope another day doesn't pass without a message. You're in luck! The radio goes off. The message:

THE WEATHER IS FOGGY IN LONDON MEET AT CAFÉ ON RUE DU BOIS SAUVAGE

You grab your hat and quickly run out the door. You know the café; it is by the church.

Turn to page 87.

The door to the testing room opens. You feel confident about your test.

"Noor," Vera approaches you with an envelope. She is not smiling.

"No, that's impossible!" You look sadly at your friend. She shakes her head.

"I'm sorry. Before you ask, Buckmaster won't give you another chance. This was already a stretch," she says as she hands you the envelope. You open it and pull out your test:

FAIL

In big red letters again.

"Maybe you're not meant for this, Noor. Maybe you should go back to your writing." Vera pats your shoulder gently. "In any case, going to Paris is extremely dangerous. Our agents have been dropping like flies over there."

"I guess so," you mumble, ignoring the mist in your eyes. You get up and leave.

The End

You shake your head. What would your father think if you chose to take the gun? Clutching your radio tightly to your chest, you give yourself a countdown:

Three.

Two.

One!

You jump up like a spring and sprint. You tumble headfirst onto the ground, your radio spilling from your hands in the process. You hear a gun click right behind your ear.

"Don't move," the guard says. "In the name of the Third Reich, you are under arrest."

Turn to page 63.

You get to the café. It is small and quaint. There are a few people sitting outside. A couple sits together at one table, holding hands. A woman in a big coat sits at the other end of the patio. A man reads a newspaper alone. You cautiously walk up to him and say, "What a lovely café on the Rue Du Bois Sauvage."

"You got my message," he says as he puts down the paper. You breathe a sigh of relief and take a seat. "I'm glad you made it to Belgium safely, Noor. You may call me Pierre." He leans in as he speaks. You try to keep your face from showing surprise— why did he use your real name? He should have called you Madeleine.

"Your message saved me from the Gestapo. Thank you, Pierre."

"I'm afraid I've only brought you into more danger." He coughs into his sleeve. "I need help from someone outside of Belgium. I can't trust anyone in the organization. That's where you come in."

"You want me to spy on the SOE here?" you gasp.

"Countless lives depend on your help. I don't want what happened in Paris to happen here in Brussels. We need to find out who the double-crosser is. You must report to me, and only to me. You cannot tell them that you are working for me. Will you do it?"

If you agree to spy on the Brussels SOE,
turn to page 91.

If you choose not to accept the mission,
turn to page 118.

"I'm not sure I'm cut out for public speaking," you say politely. "But I would love to help behind the scenes."

"Fair enough." Gandhi nods his head. "I am delighted to have your help in any way."

You spend almost a month in Bombay, joining rallies and protests, and even helping Gandhi with his speechwriting.

You've also not yet reached out to Adil. You meant to long ago, but the movement has been picking up steam and time just moves so quickly.

There is one thing that makes you curious, though, and that is Aryan. He wanders in and out of the home at all hours. He rarely ever gives a straight answer to where he's been, and today is no different.

"Aryan!" You wave to him as he walks in. "Welcome back!" He grunts a quick greeting back. "Where've you been? I haven't seen you for five days."

"You are very observant."

"Thank you, I pride myself on it."

"It's an important skill in my work."

You freeze. This is the first time Aryan has said anything about his work.

"I'm always keeping an eye out, I have to," Aryan continues. "That's basically my entire job: watching carefully and finding out what I need to know."

"You're a spy," you whisper.

"You finally figured it out. I was wondering when you would." Aryan smiles. "Were you serious about wanting to help more?"

Go on to the next page.

Suddenly you feel as though the tables have turned. Was this a test? You can see that Aryan is about to recruit you. "I have thought about it, yes," you say breathlessly.

"We are trying to find some political prisoners," he says slowly, analyzing your reaction. "Like your friend Adil."

Your heart leaps! Adil is a political prisoner? You look at Aryan and weigh your options. You don't have a stomach for violence, and you know you are doing good work writing speeches. You answer, "I'm sorry. I can't be a spy."

Aryan vanishes the next day without involving you in his work, and you return to helping Gandhi. It takes patience to write and rewrite and edit, but every time the speeches come out flawless. Support for India's freedom has grown internationally because of your hard work. Today you write about political prisoners, like Adil.

"Noor," Gandhi takes your hand gently, "never forget that you are a brilliant writer. We will find the right words. There's no one I trust more than you." Inside, you glow with pride. You never imagined you could gain the respect of someone so many hold so dear.

The End

You eye the men carefully. They certainly look guilty of something; you wonder if it has anything to do with Adil's disappearance. They keep whispering, pointing their fingers aggressively, and shaking their heads. You try to match the faces with the names of the friends Adil mentioned in his letters.

You look at the tea shop owner and nod your head. "Looks like I'm going in." You slurp down the last of your tea and head over.

When you have the opportunity, you clear your throat to get their attention. "Ahem," you say louder.

You clench your fist, then force your way into their table and take a seat on an empty stool. They look at you as if you've gone mad. "I want to know where Adil is."

"Who the heck are you?" One of them points a finger in your face. You brush it to the side.

"His mother is asking around, I'm here to help her." That's partially true.

"Hey, you!" You turn your head to see two Indian police officers coming toward the tea shop. The men jump up from the table and run.

One officer follows the man who waved his finger at you, and pounces on him. The other is coming toward you!

Turn to page 129.

Pierre waits for your answer. You take a deep breath. "Okay, I'll do it. To help save other agents."

"Thank you. Here are the coordinates to an SOE safehouse. If you radio from there, they will help you."

You nod and get up to leave.

After following Pierre's instructions, you find the location. You head inside, set up your radio, and type out your message:

THE FOG IS IN LONDON I AM AN AGENT FROM PARIS HELP MADELEINE

THERE IS FOG INDEED AGENT COMING TO RENDEZVOUS HIDE

Hours pass as you wait. The building is an abandoned store, everything already looted from the shelves. In the back you can see a small Torah, the Jewish bible, on the floor. You pick it up and put it on the table with respect, and sadness.

You hear the bell of the front door sound—one of the few things left working in the store—and you hear the light footsteps of someone making their way toward the back.

"Madeleine?"

"Elizabeth!" You jump up and embrace your friend from training days. She hugs you tightly.

"When I heard your code name, I had to come myself. I'm so glad you're safe!"

You nod, grateful to see your friend.

"But how did you find this place? This spot has been abandoned by the SOE for a while, we're pretty sure the Nazis are monitoring it."

Turn to the next page.

"I—uh." You hate lying to your friend. "I saw the Star of David on the door and thought this might be as good a place as any."

"See, I knew you were the cleverest person in our training group! Let's get out of here."

"It's crazy being in a war, isn't it," you say quietly as the two of you make your way to the hideout.

"At this point I'm not sure I remember what it's like not being in one." Elizabeth sounds different as she says this, almost bitter. You've never heard her be anything but sunny. She notices your stare and shrugs. "I'm sure we've both seen a lot. Sometimes, I can't even remember what we're fighting for, or who." You almost choke. Could Elizabeth be the traitor?

Who can you trust? Pierre was clear, there was a rat in Brussels—and it could be anyone. You test your suspicions one day and follow her.

It's a cold, rainy day, which helps you hide more. You're covered in a coat, scarf, and hat, so your face is obscured. Elizabeth practically sprints the entire way, cutting through alleyways and looping around corners. It takes every skill you have not to lose her. This is odd, even for someone undercover. Finally, she stops at a small door in a back alley. She knocks three times and then slips an envelope under the door, so it is just sticking out. Then she disappears.

Go on to the next page.

When you step up to the door you almost keel over. On the door, scratched into the wood, is a swastika! You grab the envelope and rifle through it. They're plans for the Allied troops! You tuck the envelope into your coat and head back to the hideout, choking on your tears.

You decide you must confront your friend before you meet with Pierre. "Elizabeth, tell me what's wrong," you say bluntly back at the hideout.

"I don't think you understand how things are here."

"War is terrible everywhere."

Turn to the next page.

Elizabeth blinks. "You're right. You're right, it is terrible everywhere. I'm sorry. You lost everyone working with you in France and here I am complaining."

"So, tell me what's troubling you."

"I—I—" She seems to be deciding something. "I can't tell you anything, I'm sorry. Just know that we're on the same side."

"Are we though?" you ask. You look at the time, you need to get going to meet Pierre.

"Noor," she hunches over and hugs herself. "There's just so many layers to this war. Every time I think I understand it, something else comes up. I wasn't sure how long I could keep going, but seeing you—it was like a sign! We're in this together."

You can tell there's not even the hint of a lie. She truly believes what she is saying. But what was she doing with that envelope, and a door clearly marked for Nazis?

"Elizabeth, I—" you start to say. You need to decide: who will you trust?

*If you choose to trust Elizabeth,
turn to page 120.*

*If you choose to trust Pierre,
turn to page 123.*

Vera smiles at you and hands back your test. You passed! Overcome with emotion, all she can do is hug you. You know that she is sad to see you go.

"I have a favor to ask," you say cautiously. Vera eyes you suspiciously and then sighs.

"Name it."

"I'm—I'm worried about my mother. I don't want to upset her, so I plan on telling her I'm going somewhere safer. I'm going to tell her that I'm in Africa."

"I understand, you want me to keep your real location a secret."

"Yes, and . . . and I want you to only give her good news. Please don't tell her anything bad has happened to me unless you're absolutely—"

"I will. I promise."

Turn to page 53.

"I will never help you. No matter what." Your voice is shaking, you are gripping the chair you are in so tightly your knuckles turn white. "Never."

"Wrong answer." Maurice knocks on the door three times, and the guards come in and drag you back to your cell.

Late that night, you begin to tap on the wall of your cell ever so slightly. You wait. Then you hear another prisoner tapping back, and someone else, and another. Three people are listening. You tap out your message in code:
WE NEED TO ESCAPE AT NIGHT

Another prisoner taps out:
HOW, THERE ARE GUARDS EVERYWHERE?

You tap back:
I HAVE A PLAN

You tap out the plan. They all tap back in agreement.

"Guard! Guard!" you hear one of the prisoners yell. "I will talk! I will talk! Please let me out!" You see the guard walk smugly as he passes your cell to the one next to you. He unlocks the door and—*crash!* You hear the guard's muffled cries as the prisoner next to you knocks him out. "Charles, at your service." He dangles the keys as he says this and unlocks your door.

"Good job! Now hurry and get the others. We need to move quickly!"

"I've been counting the guards and their posts since I came here," you quickly whisper to the group. "There is a stairway that isn't guarded. If we make it there, we can head down to the ground floor and find a way out from there." The others nod in agreement.

Turn to the next page.

You can't run, because the halls will echo your footsteps. Instead, you crouch in the darkness and lead the group toward the stairway. You are about to round the last corner.

"Wait!" you whisper loudly. You hear footsteps. A guard is approaching, but he's alone and you outnumber him.

"We have to knock him out before he can raise the alarm." Only three feet away from the guard is a pull alarm.

You count down to three, and then all of you leap up and run for the guard. He sees you coming and runs for the alarm. It's too late. The alarm blares. Charles knocks the guard out, and you all head to the stairway. There's no need to be cautious and quiet now. You make it to the exit.

Without a second's hesitation, you all charge for the bushes outside.

"Help!" You turn back to see Charles on the floor, holding his ankle. "Please! I can't be caught again. Please, help me! I can't run, it hurts! Please!"

The others have already disappeared into the bushes and escaped. If you keep going, you can escape too. But Charles won't make it without help.

If you keep going to save yourself, turn to page 128.

If you choose to go back and help Charles, turn to page 113.

You are alone, the only SOE agent working in Paris. Other agents have either been captured or pulled out to safety by SOE. London sent you your mission, and you've been following it: track and report Nazi movements in the city. Today you trail two Nazi guards as the sun sets. The skies are darkening with big billowing clouds, signaling it might rain. The guards make a sharp turn off the main street. Lightning cracks across the sky; thunder rumbles soon after.

After a while, moving farther and farther away from populated areas, the guards turn onto a street that is nearly abandoned, except for a large shed with some other guards standing outside it. You pull back farther. There is no way you can follow any closer without being noticed.

The guards you were following begin to shout louder to be heard over the rain. Thankfully, that means you can hear them too.

"I told you we needed our coats!" complains one guard to the other.

"Fine! Fine! You were right! Are you happy now?" the other responds.

"I'll be happy when we're done with this stupid route and are somewhere dry!"

"Be grateful we're not one of those unlucky dogs standing there. Even this cargo will be gone tomorrow, but they will have to remain standing there!"

Turn to the next page.

100

"*Heil!*" says one of the guards by the shed as if on cue. He steps forward with his arm straight out at a forty-five-degree angle, stomping one foot at the same time.

The two guards you tailed from the city stop at the shed, and a guard opens the door for him. You take the risk and get closer while they're distracted by a blinding flash of lightning. You make it just in time to see inside the shed.

It's a treasure trove of weapons and fuel cannisters.

The two guards inspect the cargo, and when they come back out, you duck down as they pass by, fading into the night. Now it is just you, the two stationed guards, and a shed stocked full of enough weapons to take down any resistance group foolhardy enough to try and overtake them. But "tomorrow"! Wasn't that what that one guard said? The weapons would be moved, and probably used, tomorrow!

You think through your options. There are only two guards here; if you move quickly and use the element of surprise, maybe you can take them down and destroy the weapons. All it would take is a well-placed shot into one of those gasoline cannisters and the whole thing will go up in flames. But maybe it's still not too late to get a message out to the SOE, so they can respond with a safer plan.

If you choose to report to headquarters in London, turn to page 106.

If you choose to try and sabotage the weapons, turn to page 109.

"Just one bite won't hurt," you whisper to yourself as your stomach growls. It's been so long since you had anything to eat, you feel faint with hunger.

But one bite turns into two, which turns into two more, which turns into five sweets. They taste heavenly! You brush the crumbs from your mouth and the table, scooting them into your hands to be thrown away before anyone—

"What have you done!" Aryan's voice booms angrily. He yanks you by the arm into a room where Gandhi is sitting with some of his followers. "She broke the strike. I saw her."

"Noor." Gandhi looks at you sadly. "I'm surprised at you and disappointed. Clearly this movement is not for you."

"I'm sorry!" You feel tears well up in your eyes.

"I'm sorry too."

You are removed from the main house and kicked out of the movement. The news of your breaking ranks spreads like wildfire. It is lonely being the odd one out.

The End

Later that night, at dinner with Adil's mother, you can't help but tell her your plan. "I'm going to help him, Auntie-ji," you say to her. You share a light meal: *paratha*, jam, and milk.

"Noor, *beti*, please don't. Let this be handled in the proper way. Don't hurt yourself." Adil's mother tries to reason with you, but you can also hear excitement in her voice. She wants to know where Adil is so badly.

"I won't hurt myself; I promise. I'm just going to see him and then I'll get him a lawyer in the morning." You don't tell her you plan to break him out tonight. Best leave it as a surprise.

When night falls, you slip in through the doors. Your mystery contact has kept the tiny one-story station unlocked after all. You suppose there isn't much that's valuable here. You head toward the back where the holding cells are. The first one is empty. The second one is empty. So is the third. Empty. Empty. Empty. No one is here. None of the officers was telling the truth! You hear someone coming in.

"She should be here. We should grab her quick and then take her to Captain Marley."

You've been set up! You find the nearest window and jump out, running back to Auntie's home.

"Well, how was he?" Adil's mother hurries you inside when you return. "Does he look well? Are they feeding him properly?"

You can't bear to look her in the eyes when you tell her. "Auntie-ji, I'm so sorry. He's not there." You hear her voice crack, and then she falls to her knees and sobs. Adil is in terrible danger.

The End

104

Dhaka is splendid. Its beauty distracts you from your mission. You spend the morning taking in the sights, trying to be inconspicuous and blend in. The address you have is the Dhakeshwari temple, an old Hindu worship site honoring the goddess the city was named after.

The temple is pale pink with bright red designs and painted white horses over the archways. You respectfully stand back from the worshipers to observe a tall statue of the goddess, with her ten arms, riding a lion and glittering brilliantly.

You leave the temple and stand outside, waiting. You're not sure what you're looking for exactly, but you feel you must be here.

Crash! Bang! You hear commotion in a nearby alleyway. It's definitely no alley cat. You head over to look. Two men have another down on the ground and are kicking him! It's Adil on the ground! Without a moment's hesitation, you jump in and push one of the men away. He trips and falls, hitting his head on the ground and stays down. This gives Adil the chance to jump up, and with two punches he knocks out the other man. You check on the first man. He's just knocked out too. You breathe a sigh of relief. Adil takes your hand and you both run away from the scene. When you get far away, you both stop running.

Go on to the next page.

"Noor?" Adil looks at you. "Noor? It really is you!" He hugs you. When you both pull away, you get a good look at him. He's scratched up, his clothes are torn. He has dark circles under his eyes. He looks like he's been through something terrible!

"What happened to you?"

"Oh, come on, you're smart enough to figure it out." He smiles and winks. Somehow, Adil is still the same playful boy you remember.

"I can guess you were working for the resistance and were captured. But how did you—"

"Escape?" His smile blooms open further. "That is a long, long story, that involves many heroic feats." He pauses. "Actually, I took the idea from one of your Jataka tales."

"You read my book?"

"Of course! And it got me out. And then here you are to save the day again! If you hadn't come along, I would have never been able to get away from those two." He gestures back in the direction you ran from.

"Why did they want to capture you so badly?"

"Because I did it. I did the impossible! I found out who the informant for the British is, and now I can tell the rest of the resistance." He takes your hand and looks deeply into your eyes. "Noor, you and your stories have saved me, and now they will save all of India!"

The End

You decide you'll report this to headquarters, rather than handling yourself. You rush back to your hideout, a room in an inn. You do odd jobs for the innkeeper in exchange for lodging. The poor woman doesn't know what you are really doing in Paris. You often feel guilty knowing that if you were found out, she would be taken to a prison camp where she would be tortured or worse.

You get to your room and pull out the radio, tapping your message in a hurry.

THE FOG IS IN LONDON URGENT NEED HELP PLEASE ANSWER MADELEINE

The storm is so heavy now it gets in the way of your signal. You keep repeating the same message over and over.

When the storm finally lifts early the next morning, you get a response from London. You go back to the shed, but when you get there everything has been moved except the guards who still stand at their post. The weapons have gone to their destination.

With anger and disappointment, you radio to London. They are pulling you out for failure. London is covered in fog the day you arrive. When you step off the plane, you see Vera waiting for you. She looks older. The war has taken its toll on her as well.

"Noor, I'm glad to see you're safe," she says, giving you a small smile.

"I'm not sure I'm glad about that," you reply, feeling your shame coil tightly around you. She puts an arm around your shoulder and walks you home.

The End

Weeks later you are on stage in front of a large crowd.

"We have the right to govern ourselves! Freedom is a right, not a privilege!" You raise your hand up and make the victory sign, ending your speech. The crowd roars wildly, chanting your name. You take a bow, then Gandhi comes up and takes your hand, raising it for all the country, the world to see. You've never felt this much pride.

You and Gandhi begin months of work. After helping Gandhi with speeches, he puts you in contact with other leaders of the movement: Nehru, Jinnah, Ambedkar. You spend more of your time with the Indian National Congress. You help write up new proclamations and decrees. You're one of the few women doing this work, but you know how to hold your own. You are meeting Gandhi for tea today.

"How are things in the Congress?" he asks.

"Slow," you answer. Gandhi laughs. "I'm trying to push for more support for reforms in women's rights and child rights. And I'm still negotiating the release of our political prisoners with the British." Aryan was the one who made you want to work on this project when he told you the truth about Adil. You think of Adil, one of the many political prisoners currently in jail. This fuels your passion for your work.

"This work seems to suit you." He lifts his cup in a small toast.

"I think I've just found my way of helping." You smile, returning the toast. "But thank you, my friend."

The End

You can't risk waiting for London to get back to you. You wait in the shadows, in the rain, for your opportunity. One of the guards leaves to relieve himself. Now's the time!

You sneak closer to the shed, winding your way behind it before stepping out of the brush. With your back against the shed wall, you slide around to the front and get behind the guard. You quietly creep behind him and, with quick movements, wrap your forearm around his throat in a sleeper hold and put a hand over his mouth. He struggles, elbowing you in the kidneys. You hold on for dear life. He starts to weaken; you can feel his body slacken underneath you. Finally, he's out cold. You drag him by the heels and dump him in some bushes far away from the shed.

The other guard comes back but doesn't see you.

"Louis?" You hear him call for his friend. "Are you in the shed again? You know you're not supposed to touch anything in there!"

He opens the shed. You can't believe your luck! You quickly crouch down and slip into the shed. It is dark.

"Louis? Come on, get out of here. Louis?" The guard stops five feet from you. You step out of the shadows. He turns! You run up and give him a firm uppercut to the chin. He falls like a stone. You laugh! These guys aren't so tough. You grab the guard's legs and drag him to his friend, then run back into the shed.

Turn to the next page.

110

You pull out one of the fuel tanks and open the top. It's too heavy to lift, so you tip it over and let some liquid leak out.

You cough from the fumes. When the tank feels lighter, you pick it up and splash all the remaining liquid onto the weapons and supplies. Then you pull another tank into the center of the shed and grab a gun. You run out of the shed, turn around at a safe distance, and aim the gun. On the first shot, you hit the tank and the whole shed goes up in flames. You look at the gun in your hand, hearing your father's voice in your head warning against violence, and then throw it into the fire. You look over at the knocked-out guards. They are still unconscious a safe distance away. You hear sirens. You need to flee!

London is extremely happy with your bravery to take charge of a difficult situation. Unfortunately, your success brings more guards out, and movement is riskier.

You steal away from the inn you were staying at in the middle of the night. Using alleyways and rooftops, you work your way to a familiar place. You haven't been here since you first left Paris all those months ago. Home.

The lights are off in all the houses, and most look abandoned. No guards, or anyone really, in sight. You walk down the street in the cool night air. Your picturesque neighborhood is now covered in litter, and there are some broken windows and doors left ajar. There are Nazi symbols everywhere. You freeze. A large Nazi flag flies from your house.

Turn to page 112.

112

You work your way to the back of your old house and test the back door. It's unlocked and creaks as it opens. You step inside and walk quietly down the halls. What's left of the furniture and your family belongings is covered in dust. Most of the furniture is gone as well as the pictures that used to hang on the walls, the vases that used to hold flowers from the garden.

You hear another set of footsteps. Someone else is here! You step cautiously toward the sound.

"Who's there?" you hear a familiar voice ask. When you round the corner, it's your old neighbor Renee! She recognizes you immediately. "Noor?"

"Renee!" You break into a smile and step closer. She holds her palm out to you and takes a step back.

"What are you doing here? I thought you left Paris!" she hisses. She sees your radio. "Where did you get that?"

"Renee, I'm so glad to see you!"

"I already contacted the Gestapo when I heard a noise. They will be here any moment," Renee says coolly. You feel sick to your stomach.

"Renee, I don't understand—" She runs toward you, ready to put up a fight.

If you choose to try to convince Renee to help you escape, turn to page 18.

If you choose to fight back, turn to page 125.

You turn back. "Charles, get up!" you yell. The alarms are deafeningly loud. Searchlights have come on, so it will only be a matter of time before they find you.

"I can't! My ankle, it hurts," he whimpers.

You slap him. Hard. "Snap out of it. You've had the same training as I have. You need to get up!" He is stunned for a moment, but you know your words have sunk in. He groans as you pull him up, leaning his weight on you. You try to move as quickly as possible. In the distance you can see the other escapees waiting. If you can get Charles to them, he'll be safe. The searchlight moves closer to your position. You pull Charles along with you as fast as you can. You are almost at the bushes.

Another escapee comes out toward you. "You are so brave. I would have left him. We almost left until we saw you turn back."

Suddenly, the sounds of warfare join the sounds of the alarms going off around you. Everyone looks to you to lead the way.

Turn to the next page.

114

There is commotion everywhere. The roar of the planes surrounds you. You look up and see they are Allies!

"Hurry! Shoot down that plane!" The commanding officer shouts at his men trying to bring order to the chaos unfolding.

"Yes sir!" some Nazi soldiers respond and then arm themselves. Flat canons and machine guns will be firing soon—you need to move quickly. You know you will have to run out into the open. You charge forward trying to get as far as you can as fast as you can.

When you glance back, you can see some other guards take notice of you, but they are too far away to catch you and the others now. You slide to a stop at the gate and push on it—it is unlocked! You lead them all out and far from the prison, now practically carrying Charles.

When you round the corner, knowing no one is coming after you in fear of the raid, you stop and take a breath. You made it! Now it's time to find a place to hide.

Turn to page 116.

116

With the others safe, you must contact London. It takes you three hours to track down the warehouse where Charles told you a radio is kept.

Inside it is dark, but you cannot risk turning on any lights. You guide yourself with your hands, reaching outward and feeling for where you are going. Finally, you feel something familiar. The hard case of the radio! You pull it off the shelf and open it. You make a wish as you turn the radio on. It works! You quickly close the case and run from the building.

Back at the hideout, you line out the aerial antenna and set up the radio. Charles is resting in the corner. You've learned the names of the other agents, Mary and Giles. They are all quite weak from months of interrogation, and you need to get them to safety.

You: THE FOG IS IN LONDON SOE IN PARIS IS DOWN I REPEAT SOE IN PARIS IS DOWN MADELEINE

London: THE FOG IS INDEED IN LONDON WILL REPORT TO HQ

You sit in the dark warehouse, ruminating over what you've just been through. This war has brought you places you could never imagine, and you must dig deep for strength to keep going. There is also a part of you that wants to get out of Paris and leave the war.

If you choose to stay, turn to page 99.

If you choose to leave, turn to page 122.

You leap back onto the buffet table. The servant sees you and screams, but it's too late. You jump up and pull yourself over the wall. When you fall to the street, you land with one foot bent under you. You howl in pain, then push yourself off the pavement and hobble away as the lights come on in the home.

When you see Priya again, she is disappointed. "I trusted you," she says ruefully.

"I'm sorry. I tried."

"Noor, if you can't do this, you can't help Adil." Priya shakes her head. "Adil is in a far more dangerous place than my uncle's home was. You should just leave."

"Leave Adil?"

"No, I mean leave India. It's clear you don't know what's going on here." As she walks away, you can feel your heart break.

The End

118

You can't lie to other agents, even for a good cause.

"There must be something else I can do to help in Brussels?"

"This is the only way to find out who is giving our secrets away. Someone betrayed you in Paris. All of the SOE agents there are gone!"

You straighten up at that response. "How could you know that all of the agents are gone?"

"I—I get my information from—"

"And how did you know where I was in Paris when you sent the message?" You remember the warning in the house. "The Gestapo came within only minutes of the message you sent. You would have had to know the exact time of the raid in advance."

"You are not listening. Belgium needs—"

"And if you knew the time of the raid in advance, why would you wait till the last possible moment to warn me? Why wouldn't you have warned HQ before the raid? You could have saved all of the agents if you wanted to."

"I tried to—"

"Stop lying." You cross your arms in front of your chest. "Who are you really?"

Go on to the next page.

"Excellent deduction, my dear." Pierre, if that is even his real name, smiles at you baring his teeth. His eyes turn mean and cold. "You have correctly guessed that I am not who I say I am."

"You work for the Nazis." Out of the corner of your eye, you glance at maybe five or six Nazi guards immediately around the café. It's a trap, and you fell right in willingly. You can feel your anger show on your face. You choose not to hide it from Pierre. Your situation looks desperate. For a second, you think of giving up. You are surrounded.

No matter what, you are your father's daughter. Just because things are hard doesn't mean you can completely let go of who you were. You know that if you let the Nazis change who you are, they have already won.

You jump up suddenly and push the table onto him. He falls with a crash, and you turn and run. You run in zigzagging lines, hearing the blur of screams and yells behind you.

Bang!

Your ears are ringing. You fall to your knees.

The End

"Elizabeth, I need to tell you something." You know it might be a risk, but you trust Elizabeth.

"What's wrong? I can see from the look on your face you're very upset."

"I saw you leave that envelope of plans for the Nazis."

"What?" Elizabeth brings a hand to her mouth. Her eyes widen with shock. "There's no way I could have, Noor—" She stops, looking hurt by your accusation. "You saw me make a drop-off, yes. But those were fake plans to find out who the spy was in our operation."

"I wasn't completely honest when I first arrived here. Please, just listen. Do you remember the store you found me in?" Elizabeth nods. You continue, "I wasn't there by chance. I was given the coordinates to message the Brussels SOE from there. I feel so stupid now. You said that day that the hideout was probably being watched by Nazis. I think the person who gave me those coordinates is working for them. An old man named Pierre."

"Oh my—oh no. I know exactly who you are talking about. I've met with him, and he sent me there," Elizabeth replies. You proceed to tell her the whole story.

Elizabeth starts to pace. You smile, remembering how she would do that back when you were training. "Pierre's been working with us for a while," she begins, "but I always had my suspicions. If he sent you to spy on us, he must be a double agent working for the Nazis. You haven't told him anything, have you?"

Go on to the next page.

"No, but I'm supposed to meet with him in an hour." You think.

"I know that look. What are you thinking?" Elizabeth smiles.

"I think I have a plan to get Pierre and save the SOE in Brussels."

You meet Pierre at a coffee shop. He is, again, pretending to read the paper. As you walk up, you notice the many Nazis casually strolling around. They are armed, and here with a purpose though they try to act otherwise.

"You made it," Pierre says. He points to the seat in front of him, but you don't take it.

"We can't talk here," you say. "Follow me, I have big news." Pierre looks up at you with surprise. He makes a small cough into his sleeve.

"Let's go." Pierre throws down his newspaper and follows you. You lead him around in crisscrossing circles, making sure no guards are following you. When the coast is clear, you lead him down to your final destination. "Where are we going? Just give me the news now!"

"The news is, you've been captured," you say as you turn to look at him and cross your arms. In that moment, Elizabeth and ten other SOE agents appear, surrounding Pierre. He offers no resistance.

You and Elizabeth are given an award for Pierre's capture, and you are ordered to London immediately.

Turn to the next page.

One morning, back in London, a surprise awaits you.

"I can't believe it!" your brother Vilayat exclaims as he hugs you. You are both in dress uniforms. "I can't believe you're here in London."

You hug him back tightly. "It's so good to see you're safe."

"Noor," he pulls away, "I can't believe you left without telling me. When I heard that you were sent to Paris, I—"

You shush him. "It's all right, dear brother. We're both safe and together again."

"Right," he smiles, "just in time for your parade!"

You blush. Since being back in London you've been receiving medals and awards for your service and saving the others, invited to dinners in your honor, and now a parade and rally to celebrate you starting in Piccadilly and ending on Parliament Street.

"You're a hero, Noor."

"Do you think Baba would be proud?" You look up at your brother shyly. You've had a hard time thinking of your father. You know Vilayat would understand.

"Of course he would be."

You walk arm in arm out the door to your hero's parade.

The End

"Yes?" Elizabeth looks at you questioningly.

"Never mind." Your cheeks turn red. How can you ignore what you saw her do?

You rush to the meeting with Pierre in time. He's waiting for you at the same café, his newspaper just as it was before.

"Pierre."

"Ah, you're just in time. Have a seat." He motions to the chair in front of him. You sit as he gives you a moment to catch your breath. You are grateful when he orders you tea and some biscuits.

"I have the information you wanted and more," you say, and you slip him Elizabeth's envelope. "There's something odd going on for sure. Something is going to happen soon." You drain your tea.

"Oh Noor. You fool!"

Pierre's words confuse you. The world starts to spin and you try to stand, but you're too dizzy. You try to open your mouth to speak but can't. There was something in the tea!

"Guards!" Pierre calls as he takes the envelope you brought. "Arrest her in the name of the Third Reich!"

"You're the trai—" You barely finish the sentence before you fall unconscious. Now Belgium is lost too.

The End

124

"I'll do it," you whisper. "I will tell you how the code works."

"Good choice," Maurice answers, then whispers something to another guard before turning back to you. You proceed to answer all of his questions. You hold nothing back. Then, without warning you are pulled out of your seat. "Let's go."

The guards drag you down hallway after hallway until you reach a small room. You're pushed in, alongside everyone from Paris headquarters. A guard walks in with a gun. "You said they'd be safe!"

The interrogator shrugs. "I lied."

The End

You lunge at Renee, but she pushes you down, kicking and punching you. Each blow comes down like a hammer. You can't get her off. Desperate, you dive to the side and grab a heavy iron door stop. You smash it against her skull, knowing you've killed her.

Despite knowing you acted in self-defense, tears of guilt and sadness stream down your face. Renee was once a friend. The sirens sound distant, everything is foggy. You look at what you did one last time and run, making it out before the Gestapo arrive.

It is a week before SOE can smuggle you out of Paris. When you return to London, you decide to stay in your own apartment instead of with your family. You've changed, and you can't bear for them to see it. Your nights are filled with haunting images of the war, filled with the things you did or almost did. You are haunted by the eyes you closed forever.

The End

126

"I need to live," you tell yourself. You take the gun and scoot yourself farther away from the dumpster. You look one more time. If you can run toward the guard and avoid being shot, you've got a chance. You squat in position, gun in one hand, the radio in the other, and give yourself a countdown:

Three.

Two.

One!

You sprint in zigzagging lines and keep your head down. You run so fast you feel like you could fall over at any moment, but you don't. You shoot at the guard, hitting him in the knee. He falls to the side, and you make it out.

You run away as fast as you can for as long as you can, never once looking back. Everyone is lost. When you finally feel safe, you look at the gun in your hand with disgust and throw it in a nearby ditch, ashamed of yourself.

Go on to the next page.

You're thankful you still have your radio after everything. You set it up and quickly tap out a message:

THE FOG IS IN LONDON NEED HELP SOE OPERATIONS IN PARIS DOWN

You wait for the return message.

THE FOG IS INDEED IN LONDON PLEASE REPEAT ALL OF PARIS DOWN
YES NAZIS HAVE CAPTURED EVERYONE ELSE THIS IS MADELEINE

The line is silent. They must be deciding what to do . . .

NEED PERSON ON THE GROUND IN PARIS BUT CAN TAKE YOU BACK TO LONDON

You are stunned. You didn't even think it would be possible to get you out of mainland Europe now. If you choose to stay, you'd be working alone in Paris. If not, you could be back in London, safe.

You rub your forehead with both hands. What you wouldn't give to feel safe!

If you choose to return to London,
turn to page 43.

If you choose to work in Paris as the only SOE
agent, turn to page 99.

You mouth an apology and keep running. You can't risk going back to him.

"Curse you!" Charles screams. "You traitor! You're leaving me here to die! I'm going to die!"

You try your best to ignore his words as you run, but they echo in your head. You make it to the bushes and hide. You can't help yourself, but you look back at Charles on the ground, surrounded by guards.

"Pick him up!" one yells at the others. Charles screams in pain. A guard kicks his ankle, sending another scream from Charles's lips. They drag him back inside, and you slip away. The other prisoners have scattered, leaving you alone.

Hours later, sitting in your safehouse, you can't believe you're alive. You managed to get away from the Nazis but can't stop hearing Charles's last words to you ringing in your head.

You are desperate. After tracking down a radio, you are able to send a message. You radio London:

THE FOG IS IN LONDON I CAN'T DO THIS PLEASE TAKE ME OUT OF PARIS

You wait a long time; it feels like ages.

WE WILL GET YOU OUT

Finally back in London, you become a recluse. The war has left many scars on you, both physical and mental, but the worst part is remembering what you did over and over again. You have nightmares. You cannot sleep through a whole night.

The End

You dash out of the tea shop, away from the officer as he closes in. Pushing through the crowd, you make it a good distance away before you feel something bash into your head. The world spins around you, you feel yourself falling, and everything goes black.

You rub your eyes. Your head hurts badly and the ringing in your ears won't stop. Was it all a bad dream? When you open your eyes, you don't recognize your surroundings. You are in a small cot, there is a sink on one wall and a bucket, and then you see the jail cell bars.

"No!" You get up and go to the jail cell door. "Hey! Hey! I don't belong here! I did nothing wrong!"

"Noor?" You look across from your cell into another. It's Priya! "What are you doing here?"

"Me? What are you doing in Lahore? In jail?" You see a sadness in her eyes.

"We're not in Lahore anymore."

"What?"

"You never went to see that contact in Amritsar, did you?" Priya shakes her head. "Now we're lost just like Adil."

"What do you mean?"

"I mean that we've been captured as secret political prisoners for working to free India." A tear falls down Priya's face. "We're never getting out."

The End

GLOSSARY

Auntie-ji and **Gandhi-ji** – Why was "-ji" added at the end of Gandhi and Noor's Auntie's name? The addition of *-ji* at the end of someone's name is a sign of respect for that person.

Beti – The Hindi word for daughter.

Bhai – The Hindi word for brother.

Biryani – An Indian dish made of rice and warming spices, typically served with meat or hard boiled egg, saffron, yogurt, and crispy onions.

Chai wallah – A *chai wallah* is someone who makes, sells, and serves tea.

Dupatta – A *dupatta* is a scarf, and is typically worn with a *shalwar kamiz*.

Ek – The Urdu word for one.

Gandhi – Born in 1869, Mahatma Gandhi was an Indian activist who peacefully fought for Indian independence, non-violence, and civil rights. Gandhi was a pacifist, who believed in tolerance for all. He studied law, and practiced for a short time. Gandhi was imprisoned many times for fighting for what he believed in. He was tragically assassinated in 1948 at the age of 78.

Henna – Henna is a plant based ingredient that was originally used to stain fingernails, which showed one's social status. It is more commonly used to paint on people's hands and feet for ceremonies.

Karo ya maro – *Karo ya maro* was said by Gandhi during a speech in 1942. It means "do or die."

Kohl – Thought to be originally used for either eye protection from the sun or as a symbol of one's high social status. Kohl is a black powder worn around the eyes, as make-up.

Kon – The Urdu word for who.

Kulfi – A traditional Indian ice cream. It is often served on a popsicle stick in the shape of a cone. It is commonly flavored with mango or pistachio.

Mandap – The Hindi word for pavilion. A *mandap* is brightly colored and decorated with flowers. It has four pillars and is where the couple will stand when they get married.

Naan – Indian leavened bread, meaning a rising ingredient like yeast will be used to make this bread. It is typically oval in shape and is flat. *Naan* is traditionally cooked in a tandoor, which is a type of oven.

Lehnga – A traditional Indian full length skirt. It is typically embroidered and pleated.

Palak Paneer – An Indian dish made with spinach and cheese (*palak:* spinach; *paneer:* cheese).

Paratha – *Paratha* is another type of Indian bread. It is different from *naan* because it is not leavened. *Paratha* is cooked in a frying pan rather than in an oven. It is a flat bread that can be eaten on its own or can be stuffed with fillings.

Raita – A Southern Asian dish made of yogurt, cucumber, and mint leaf.

Salam – The Urdu way to greet someone.

Shaadi – The Hindi word for wedding.

Shalwar kamiz – *Shalwar* are loose trousers and a *kamiz* is a tunic. The two are traditionally worn together as one outfit.

Shukriya – The Hindi word for thank you.

SOE – SOE stands for the Special Operations Executive. Created in 1940 by the British, the SOE was a secret program used for training people to become spies during World War II.

The Story of Noor Inayat Khan

Noor-un-Nissa Inayat Khan was born January 1, 1914, in Moscow, Russia. Noor and her family moved from Russia to London just before World War I, and then to France when Noor was six years old.

Noor's parents met when her father traveled to the United States to teach. Noor's mother, Nora Baker, who changed her name to Pirani Ameena Begum, was born in the United States, in New Mexico, and was raised studying yoga and music. Inayat Khan, Noor's father, grew up in India. He was descended from the royal family of the Kingdom of Mysore. Noor's father was a musician and a teacher of Sufism, a religion dating back to the eleventh-century in Central Asia, India, and parts of Europe and Africa. He believed strongly in nonviolence. The pair had four children, and Noor was the oldest.

Noor grew up surrounded by the lessons her parents valued: nonviolence, music, writing, and the arts. When Noor's father died in 1927, Noor cared for all in her family while beginning a career as a children's book writer and poet. She studied child psychology at the Sorbonne and harp and piano music at the Paris Conservatory.

The outbreak of World War II destroyed Noor's family home. Her once-peaceful neighborhood was invaded by Nazi forces, and families were forced to evacuate. While most of her family fled for safety, Noor and her brother Vilayat decided to fight back on the side of the Allies, those who fought against the Nazis (the "Axis") during the war. World War II was violent and scary for everyone who lived in Europe, and in other nations. In Europe, the Nazi leader Adolf Hitler's evil was greater than only military threat. He and the Nazi party murdered millions of Jewish people, and many lives were lost, soldiers and civilians both.

War even reached Noor and Vilayat's father's homeland in India, where new problems formed between Indian people who wanted to break free of British rule, while the British military hoped India would help it fight the war.

Noor joined the Women's Auxiliary Air Force in 1940 when she was only twenty-six years old. She worked for the Special Operations Executive (SOE), a secret organization dedicated to spying. Many of the people Noor meets in this book are real people who worked as spies in World War II. Vera Atkins led Noor and then many other women through their dangerous spying assignments. We will never know the whole story of what happened to Noor or many of the spies she worked with, as their work was secret.

Noor's code name was Madeleine, so her real identity was kept secret. She was trained to use wireless radios that were used to pass secret messages for the Allied forces. After three years of training, Noor was the first woman sent into the enemy territory as a radio operator. Her mission was to survive amidst the Nazi soldiers undetected, listening and spying and transmitting messages back to the Allies on her radio. The work was important and incredibly dangerous.

The messages Noor transmitted during the war were of the highest level of secrecy and importance. She was responsible for sending messages about sabotage, weapons location, and plans of violence. She had to hide not just herself but also the long coil of aerial antenna she used to boost the signal.

As Noor's job grew more dangerous, her brother Vilayat turned to their father's nonviolent beliefs. He decided he could no longer support the violent, dangerous war, and he urged Noor to join him in safety. Noor's superiors at the SOE were also worried about the great danger she was taking on, but Noor insisted that she remain on her mission, asking her bosses to send her family good news about her work and to keep them safe.

Noor returned to France and joined other spies in the SOE. One of these spies betrayed her to the Nazis, and she was captured. During her capture, Noor remained brave and stuck with her training. She gave up no information even under interrogation. Noor escaped the headquarters of the Nazi intelligence agency, the SD, with two other spies. She was captured again, now considered "highly dangerous." She was kept prisoner for almost a year, and continued to refuse to give up any information.

Noor was executed at Dachau concentration camp in Germany by a Nazi soldier. Her last word was "*Liberté.*" After her death, she was honored with the George Cross for her work as a spy. She died September 13, 1944, when she was only thirty years old.

Today, Noor is remembered for her bravery. She defied not only the soldiers who captured her but the expectations nearly everyone had for her and her future. She had opportunities to stay safe and avoid the war. The lessons of her father and her religion taught her the value of nonviolence. And yet, Noor stepped up to fight against evil because she knew it was right, even if it meant leaving behind everything familiar to her.

ABOUT THE ARTISTS

Illustrator: Laurence Peguy was born in the South of France. After her Baccalaureate, she graduated from the Emile Cohl Art School in Lyon. She is currently working in the film industry as a texture artist and has participated in projects including the *Golden Compass, Monster in Paris, Dr Seuss' the Lorax, White Fang* . . .
She is also an illustrator working on her own projects (and this is her third *Choose Your Own Adventure* book).

Cover Artist: Mia Marie Overgaard has been working as a professional artist since graduating from the Royal Danish Academy of Architecture's School of Design in 2006. Mia's creative curiosity has allowed her to span a variety of media and creative fields — from illustration to fashion, graphic design, and fine art. Mia's distinctive illustrations have appeared in numerous books and publications worldwide, and have been exhibited in various locations around the globe such as London, Paris, Estonia, Georgia, Hungary, Sweden, Denmark, and Tokyo.

ABOUT THE AUTHOR

Rana Tahir is a Kundiman Fellow, a public school substitute teacher, and a teaching associate in the Department of English at Pacific University in Forest Grove, Oregon, where she earned her MFA. She was born in Pakistan and raised on the beaches of Kuwait. Tahir's poetry and prose have been published in various literary publications and magazines such as *Catch, The Interlochen Review,* and *Fresh! Literary Magazine*. Her first book of non-fiction, a biography of the poet Countée Cullen, was published in 2016 with Cavendish Square Press. She is excited to return to Portland, Oregon, with her husband and hopes to be joined by a cat soon. When not at her desk preparing lesson plans, writing, or researching, she can be found jumping into lakes and rivers during long hikes, even though she always forgets a bathing suit and must sit in the car in her cold, wet clothes on the ride home. She is a Cancer sun and moon, so she never regrets being in water.

For games, activities, and other fun stuff, or to write to Rana, visit us online at CYOA.com

NOOR INAYAT KHAN

This book is different from other books. YOU and you alone are in charge of what happens in this story.

Your name is Noor Inayat Khan, and you have a secret royal heritage. You live with your family in a beautiful home in France, where you write poetry and children's books. You study music and can speak many languages. Everything for you and your family changes with World War II.

News hits that the Nazis have come to France and YOU have a big decision to make. You were raised with pacifist beliefs but you see how important it is to help with the war efforts. Will you escape to India, your father's homeland? Or will you remain in Europe and find a way to help with the war? You will also make choices that determine YOUR own fate in the story. Choose carefully because the wrong choice could end in disaster—even death. But don't despair. At any time, YOU can go back and make another choice, and alter the path of your fate . . . and maybe even history.